The BOOK of PROPER NAMES

The BOOK of PROPER NAMES

Amélie Nothomb

TRANSLATED FROM THE FRENCH
BY SHAUN WHITESIDE

St. Martin's Press

New York

THE BOOK OF PROPER NAMES. Copyright © 2002 by Editions Albin Michel, S.A. Translation copyright © 2004 by Shaun Whiteside. All rights reserved. Printed in the United States of America. No part of this book may be used or reproduced in any manner whatsoever without written permission except in the case of brief quotations embodied in critical articles or reviews. For information, address St. Martin's Press, 175 Fifth Avenue, New York, N.Y. 10010.

First published in France under the title *Robert des noms propres* by Editions Albin Michel, S.A.

www.stmartins.com

Library of Congress Cataloging-in-Publication Data

Nothomb, Amélie.
    [Robert des noms propres. English]
    The book of proper names / Amélie Nothomb.— 1st U.S. ed.
        p. cm.
    ISBN 0-312-32055-8
    EAN 978-0312-32055-3
    1. Title.
PQ2674.O778R6313 2004
843'.914—dc22

                                                                2004006097

First U.S. Edition: August 2004

10   9   8   7   6   5   4   3   2   1

The BOOK of PROPER NAMES

LUCETTE HAD BEEN suffering from insomnia for eight hours. The baby in her womb had been hiccuping since the day before. Every four or five seconds a huge jolt shook the small body of the nineteen-year-old girl.

She had decided to become a wife and mother a year before. It had begun like a dream: Fabien was handsome and said he was willing to do anything for her. Playing at marriage had amused him. Her family, simultaneously puzzled and touched, had watched these two children put on their wedding outfits.

Shortly afterwards, Lucette had triumphantly announced that she was pregnant.

Her big sister had asked her, "Isn't it kind of soon?"

"It'll never be soon enough!" the girl replied, deliriously.

LITTLE BY LITTLE things soured. Fabien and Lucette argued. Where once he had been so happy about her pregnancy, now he said, "I hope you're not going to go crazy when you've got a kid!"

"Are you threatening me?"

He went out, slamming the door.

Lucette was sure she wasn't crazy. She wanted life to be strong and rich. Wouldn't you have had to be crazy to want anything else? She wanted every day, every year, to bring her the absolute maximum.

Now she could see that Fabien wasn't the right guy for her. He was an ordinary kid. He had played at getting married, and now he was playing at being a married man. There was nothing of the Prince Charming about him. In fact, he repelled her. He said things like, "Okay, she's having a fit."

He could be nice sometimes. He would stroke her belly, saying, "If it's a boy, we'll name him Tanguy. If it's a girl, it'll be Joëlle."

Lucette was thinking that she hated those names.

In her grandfather's library she had picked up an old encyclopedia with lists of phantasmagorical first names,

names that bespoke *destinies*. Lucette conscientiously jotted them down on bits of paper that she sometimes lost. Later, people would find scattered around the place scraps of paper bearing the word "Eleuthère" or "Lutegarde." No one could guess the meaning of these cryptic and surreal messages.

THE BABY HAD started to move very quickly. The gynecologist said he had never before encountered such an active fetus. "It's unbelievable!"

Lucette smiled. Her child was exceptional already. All this took place in those recent times when it was not yet possible to know the child's sex in advance. The pregnant girl didn't care.

"Whichever sex it is, it's going to be a dancer," she decreed, her head full of dreams.

"No," said Fabien, "it's going to be a soccer player or a pain in the ass."

She looked daggers at him. He meant nothing by it, it was just a tease. But in such childish observations, she saw the mark of insurmountable vulgarity.

When she was on her own and the fetus moved like a thing possessed, she would speak tenderly to it: "Go on, dance, my baby. I'll protect you, I won't let you be a soccer-playing Tanguy or a pain-in-the-ass Joëlle.

3

You'll be free to dance wherever you like, at the Paris Opera, or for little bands of gypsies."

GRADUALLY, FABIEN HAD taken to disappearing for whole afternoons. He left after lunch and came back at about ten in the evening, without a word of explanation. Exhausted by her pregnancy, Lucette didn't have the strength to wait for him. She was already asleep by the time he came back. In the morning he stayed in bed until half past eleven. He drank coffee with a cigarette, which he smoked as he stared into the void.

"Are you all right? Not tiring yourself out?" she asked him one day.

"What about you?" he replied.

"I'm having a baby. You aware of that?"

"How could I not be? It's the only thing you ever talk about."

"Believe me, it's exhausting, being pregnant."

"That's not my fault. You're the one who wanted it. I can't carry the thing for you."

"Any chance of knowing what you do every afternoon?"

"No."

She exploded with rage. "I don't know anything anymore! You never tell me a thing!"

4

"You're not interested in anything apart from the baby."

"All you have to do is be interesting. Then I'll be interested in you."

"I *am* interesting."

"Okay, then let's see if you can be."

He sighed and went off to get a box. Out of it he took a handgun. She opened her eyes wide.

"That's what I do in the afternoon. I shoot."

"Where do you do that?"

"A private club. It doesn't matter."

"Are there real bullets in there?"

"Yes."

"For killing people?"

"Among other things."

She stroked the gun, fascinated.

"I'm getting good, you know. I get the bull's-eye first time. You can't imagine how good it feels. I love it. Once I get started I can't stop."

"I can understand that."

They didn't understand each other often.

LUCETTE'S BIG SISTER, who had two small children, came to see Lucette. She adored her. She thought she was so pretty, so frail, especially with that enormous belly. One day they had an argument.

5

"You should tell him to go out and get a job. He's going to be a father."

"We're nineteen. Our parents pay for everything."

"They won't go on paying forever."

"Why are you bothering me with all this nonsense?"

"It's important, you know."

"You always come and ruin my happiness!"

"What are you talking about?"

"And now you're going to tell me I have to be sensible blah blah blah!"

"You're crazy! I haven't said anything of the sort!"

"That's it! I'm crazy! That's just what I was expecting you'd say! You're jealous of me! You want to destroy me!"

"Come on, Lucette . . ."

"Get out!" she screamed.

Her big sister left, aghast. She had always known that her baby sister was fragile, but things were assuming worrisome proportions.

From now on, when her sister called, Lucette hung up the moment she heard her voice.

I've got enough problems, she thought to herself.

In fact, without admitting it, she felt that she was up against the wall, and that her big sister knew that. How would they ever earn a living? Fabien wasn't interested in anything except guns, and she wasn't good at anything. Nonetheless, she wasn't going to be a checkout girl. She wasn't sure she was up to it.

She put a pillow over her head to stop thinking about it.

SO THAT NIGHT the baby had hiccups in Lucette's belly.

You can't imagine the impact a hiccuping fetus has on a pregnant girl with ragged nerves.

Fabien was blissfully asleep.

Lucette was in her eighth hour of insomnia and her eighth month of pregnancy. Her vast belly made her feel as though she held a time bomb inside her.

Each hiccup was like a timer ticking, bringing the moment of the detonation ever closer. Fantasy became reality: something exploded inside Lucette's head.

She got up, driven by a sudden conviction that made her open her eyes wide.

She went to get the revolver from where Fabien had hidden it. She came back toward the bed where the boy was sleeping. She looked at his handsome face as she aimed at his temple and murmured, "I love you, but I've got to protect the baby from you."

She fired until the magazine was empty.

She looked at the blood on the wall. Then, very calmly, she called the police. "I just killed my husband. You'd better come."

. . .

WHEN THE POLICE arrived, they were welcomed by a child, pregnant up to the eyeballs, a handgun in her right hand.

"Put down the weapon!"

"It's not loaded now," she replied, obeying.

She led the policemen over to the marriage bed to show them her work.

"Should we take her to the station or to the hospital?"

"Why the hospital? There's nothing wrong with me."

"We don't know that. And you're pregnant."

"I'm not about to give birth. Take me to the police station," she demanded, as though it were her right.

She was told that she could call a lawyer. She said there was no need. A man in an office asked her endless questions, which she answered, such as:

"Why did you kill your husband?"

"The baby in my belly had hiccups."

"And?"

"That's it. I killed him."

"You killed him because the baby had hiccups?"

She looked taken aback, then answered, "No. It's not as simple as that. And anyway, the baby doesn't have hiccups anymore."

"You killed your husband to get rid of your baby's hiccups?"

She laughed. "No, that would be absurd."

"Why did you kill your husband?"

"To protect my baby," she said, assuming a tragic expression.

"I see. Your husband threatened the baby?"

"Yes."

"You should have said so right away."

"Yes."

"And what did he threaten it with?"

"He wanted to call it Tanguy if it was a boy and Joëlle if it was a girl."

"What else?"

"That's it."

"You killed your husband because you didn't like the first names he chose?"

She frowned. She felt her argument lacked a certain something, and yet she was sure she was right. She understood perfectly what she had done, and found it all the more frustrating that she couldn't explain it. So she decided to say nothing.

"Are you sure you don't want a lawyer?"

She was sure. How could she have explained it to a lawyer? He would have thought she was a lunatic, like everyone else. The more she spoke, the more people

9

thought she was a lunatic. That being the case, she'd keep her mouth shut.

SHE WAS PUT in a cell. A nurse came to see her every day.

When she was told that her mother or her big sister had come to visit, she refused to see them.

She answered only questions about her pregnancy. Apart from that, she stayed mute.

She talked to herself: *I was right to kill Fabien. He wasn't bad, he was mediocre. The only thing about him that wasn't mediocre was his handgun, but he would only have used it in a mediocre way, against the little local thugs, or else he'd have let the baby play with it. I was right to turn it on him. Wanting to call your child "Tanguy" or "Joëlle" is the same as offering them a mediocre world, a closed horizon. I want my baby to have infinity within its reach. I want my child not to feel limited by anything at all, I want my baby's first name to suggest that its fate will be exceptional.*

LUCETTE GAVE BIRTH to a little girl in prison. She took her in her arms and looked at her with all the love in the world. No one had ever seen a more delighted young mother.

"You're too beautiful!" she told the baby, over and over again.

"What are you going to call her?"

"Plectrude."

A delegation of wardens, psychologists, vague-looking lawyers, and even vaguer-looking doctors crowded around Lucette and told her that she couldn't give her daughter a name like that.

"Yes, I can. There was a Saint Plectrude. I can't remember what she did, but she did exist."

A specialist was consulted, and confirmed this as the truth.

"Think of the child, Lucette."

"That's all I am thinking about."

"It'll only cause her problems."

"It will tell people that she's exceptional."

"You can be called Marie and be exceptional."

" 'Marie' doesn't protect you. 'Plectrude' protects you. That 'rude' at the end sounds like a shield."

"So call her Gertrude, then. It's easier to deal with."

"No. The first part of 'Plectrude' sounds like 'pectoral.' The name is a talisman."

"The name is grotesque and your child will be a laughingstock."

"No. It will make her strong enough to defend herself."

"Why give her reason to have to defend herself? She's going to have enough problems to deal with anyway!"

"Are you referring to me?"

"Among other things."

"Don't worry, I don't intend to trouble her for long. Listen to me. I'm in prison, I'm deprived of my rights. The only freedom I have left is to name my child as I wish."

"That's selfish, Lucette."

"Just the opposite. And anyway, it has nothing to do with you."

She had the baby baptized in prison so that she could be sure of controlling everything.

That very night she made a rope from some torn sheets and hanged herself in her cell. They found her weightless corpse in the morning. She hadn't left a letter or an explanation. Her daughter's first name took the place of a will.

CLÉMENCE, LUCETTE'S OLDER sister, came to the prison to get the baby. The authorities were only too happy to get rid of the child, born under such horribly inauspicious circumstances.

Clémence and her husband, Denis, had two children, aged four and two, Nicole and Béatrice. They decided that Plectrude would be their third.

Nicole and Béatrice came to look at their new sister. They had no reason to think that she was Lucette's daughter. And, anyway, they had barely been aware of Lucette's existence.

They were too little to realize that she had a weird name, and though they had problems with the pronunciation, they adopted her. For a long time they called her "Plecrude."

Never had anyone seen a baby more skilled at attracting love. It was as if she were aware that she had been born under tragic circumstances. With heartrending glances she begged those around her to disregard the fact. It helped that she had improbably beautiful eyes. Small and thin, she fixed upon her target her vast gaze—vast in both size and meaning. Her huge, magnificent eyes told Clémence and Denis: Love me! Your destiny is to love me! I'm only eight weeks old, but I'm still a magnificent creature! If you knew, if you only knew. . . .

Denis and Clémence seemed to know. From the very first, they felt a sort of awe for Plectrude. Everything about her was strange, from the unbearable slowness with which she drank from her bottle, to the way she never cried, the fact that she slept little at night and a great deal during the day, or the way she pointed a resolute finger at things she craved.

She looked seriously, profoundly, at anyone who picked her up, as though to say that this was the beginning of a great love story, and that they had every reason to be stirred to their souls.

CLÉMENCE, WHO HAD loved her late sister to distraction, transferred her passion to Plectrude. She didn't love her any more than she did her own two children: she loved her in a different way. Nicole and Béatrice inspired an overwhelming tenderness in her; Plectrude inspired veneration.

Her two elder daughters were pretty, sweet, intelligent, agreeable; the little one was extraordinary—splendid, intense, enigmatic, crazy.

Denis was also wild about her right from the start, and he remained so. But nothing could match the love Clémence felt for her. There was wild passion between Lucette's sister and her daughter.

Plectrude had no appetite, and she grew as slowly as she ate. Her parents felt desperate. Nicole and Béatrice devoured and grew before their very eyes. To their parents' delight, they had round, pink cheeks. As for Plectrude, all that grew was her eyes.

"ARE WE REALLY going to call her that?" Denis asked Clémence one day.

"Of course. My sister insisted on the name."

"Your sister was crazy."

"No. My sister was fragile. Anyway, I think 'Plectrude' is pretty."

"Really?"

"Yes. And it suits her."

"I don't agree. She looks like a fairy. I'd have called her 'Aurora.'"

"It's too late. The girls have already adopted her under her real name. Believe me, it does suit her. It's like the name of a gothic princess."

"Poor kid. Things are going to be hard at school."

"Not for her. She has enough personality to cope."

PLECTRUDE UTTERED HER first word at a normal age. It was "Mama!"

Clémence went into ecstasies. Laughing, Denis pointed out that the first word of all her children—and all the children in the world—was "mama."

"This is different," said Clémence.

"Mama" was Plectrude's only word for a very long time. This word was, like the umbilical cord, sufficient connection with the world. From the first, she had pronounced the word perfectly, in a confident voice and with a clear "ah" sound at the end, unlike the *mamamamam* of most babies.

She uttered the word rarely, but when she did it was with a solemn clarity that commanded attention. You would have sworn that she chose her moments for maximum effect.

Clémence had been six when Lucette was born: she remembered very clearly what her sister had been like at birth, at the age of one, at two, and so on.

"Lucette was ordinary. She cried a lot, she was alternately adorable and unbearable. There was nothing special about her. Plectrude is nothing like her. She's silent, serious, thoughtful. You can sense how intelligent she is."

Denis gently mocked his wife: "Stop talking about her as though she were the second coming. She's a charming child, that's all."

He lifted Plectrude up above his head, his heart melting.

MUCH LATER, PLECTRUDE said, "Papa."

The next day, out of pure diplomacy, she said, "Nicole" and "Béatrice."

Her pronunciation was impeccable.

She started speaking as parsimoniously as she ate. Each new word demanded as much concentration and meditation as the new types of food that appeared on her plate.

Whenever she saw an unfamiliar vegetable in the

depths of her mashed potato, she pointed it out to Clémence.

"That?" she asked.

"That's leek. *Leek*. You try it, it's very good."

Plectrude first of all spent half an hour contemplating the piece of leek in her spoon. She brought it up to her nose to gauge its scent, then she went on studying it for ages and ages.

"Now it's cold!" said Denis, crossly.

She didn't care. When she decided it was time to conclude her examination, she took the food in her mouth and let it sit there. She delivered no verdict. She began the experiment over again with a second piece, then a third. The most astonishing thing was that she continued in this fashion even when her final judgment, after four attempts, was: "I hate it."

Normally, when a child hates some food, he knows it the minute it touches his tongue. Plectrude, on the other hand, wanted to be sure.

It was the same with words; she stored any verbal novelties inside her and examined them from every angle before taking them out again, most often out of context and to everyone's surprise: "Giraffe!"

Why did she say "giraffe" when they were preparing to go out for a walk? She was suspected of not understanding her own declarations. Yet she did understand.

17

It was just that her thoughts were independent of external contingencies. All of a sudden, just as she was slipping on her coat, Plectrude's mind had finished digesting the vastness of the neck and feet of the giraffe. So she had to utter its name, to alert people to the emergence of the giraffe within her internal universe.

"Have you noticed how lovely her voice is?" said Clémence.

"Have you ever heard a child who didn't have a pretty voice?" observed Denis.

"Exactly! Her voice isn't pretty, it's lovely," she replied.

IN SEPTEMBER SHE was sent to nursery school.

"She'll be three in a month. It might be a bit early."

That wasn't the problem.

After a few days, the teacher told Clémence that she couldn't keep Plectrude.

"She's too little, isn't she?"

"No, that's not it. I've got children younger than she in the class."

"So?"

"It's because of her eyes."

"What?"

"She makes the other children cry just by staring at them. And I have to say that I understand them. *I* feel uneasy when she stares at me."

Clémence, filled with pride, announced to everyone that her daughter had been expelled from nursery school because of her eyes. No one had ever heard anything like it.

PEOPLE WERE ALREADY murmuring, "Have you ever heard of a child being kicked out of nursery school?"

"And because of their eyes!"

"That kid does have a funny way of staring at you!"

"The two older ones are so well behaved, so nice. She's a little demon!"

Clémence was careful not to ask her neighbors whether they knew the circumstances of her birth. She preferred to think that people assumed Plectrude was hers.

She was delighted that she was remaining so close to the child. In the morning, Denis went off for work, driving the two older children, one to school and the other to nursery school. Clémence stayed alone with the last little girl.

As soon as the door closed on her husband and children, she transformed into another person. She became the composite of fairy and witch that Plectrude's presence awoke within her.

"The coast is clear. Let's go change."

She changed in the most profound sense of that

word; not only did she swap her normal clothes for luxurious fabrics that made her look like an Indian queen, she swapped her maternal soul for that of a phantasmagoric creature with exceptional powers.

Under the child's steady gaze, the twenty-eight-year-old liberated from within her breast the youthful fairy and the ageless witch that dwelt there.

Then she undressed the child and clothed her in a princess's dress she had secretly bought for her. She took her by the hand and led her to the big mirror, where they contemplated themselves.

"Have you seen how beautiful we are?"

Plectrude sighed with happiness.

Clémence danced. Plectrude joined in delightedly. Clémence held her hands, then suddenly grabbed Plectrude by the waist and made her fly through the air. Plectrude uttered cries of joy.

"Now look at the things," demanded the child. This was part of the ritual.

"What things?" asked Clémence, pretending not to know.

"The princess things."

THE PRINCESS THINGS were the objects which, for one reason or another, had been selected as noble, magnificent, unusual, or rare—worthy, in fact, of the admiration of such an august person as this little girl.

On the oriental carpet in the drawing room Clémence gathered together her old jewels; carmine velvet slippers that she had worn for only a single evening; a lorgnette, its lenses set in a gold art nouveau frame; a silver cigarette box; a brass Middle Eastern flask encrusted with large fake stones; a pair of white lace gloves; gaudy plastic medieval-looking rings from a toy dispenser; and a gold cardboard crown.

They had before them a pile of the most disparate yet marvelous objects. With your eyes half closed, you would have said it was a real treasure trove.

Mouth agape, the little girl stared at this pirate booty. She picked up each object in turn and studied it with ecstatic gravity.

Sometimes Clémence would dress her up in all the jewels and the slippers; then she handed her the lorgnette and said, "Now you can see how beautiful you are."

Holding her breath, the little girl looked at her reflection in the mirror: staring through the gilded circles she discovered a queen, a brightly-colored priestess, a Persian bride on her wedding day, a Byzantine saint posing for an icon. Inside all of these images she recognized herself.

Anyone might have burst out laughing at the sight of this tiny child, decked out like some insane reliquary. Clémence smiled but didn't laugh. What struck her, more than the comedy of the scene, was the beauty of the little girl. She was as beautiful as the engravings you saw in antique fairy-tale storybooks.

"Children today aren't as beautiful as that," she thought, absurdly—the children of the past were surely no better.

She put on some "princess music"—Tchaikovsky, Prokofiev—and prepared a lunch of gingerbread, chocolate cupcakes, apple turnovers, amaretti biscuits, flan, and, to drink, sweet cider and almond syrup.

Clémence spread these treats out on the table feeling a mixture of amusement and guilt. She would never have allowed her two older daughters to eat only sweets. She justified herself by reflecting that Plectrude was different: "It's a meal for fairy-tale children."

She closed the curtains, lit candles, and called Plectrude in. The little girl barely nibbled, listening with big, attentive eyes to what her mother told her.

AT ABOUT TWO O'CLOCK in the afternoon, Clémence suddenly realized that the older girls would be coming back in barely three hours, and that she had to fulfill the tasks that a mother has to perform.

Then she jumped into her ordinary clothes, ran to the corner shop to buy proper food, came back to get the apartment looking halfway decent, threw the dirty laundry into the washing machine, and then set off for school to get the children. In her haste, she didn't always remove Plectrude's disguise—for the simple reason that, in her eyes, it wasn't a disguise.

So what people saw was a cheerful young woman walking along the street, holding by the hand a tiny creature looking like the princesses in *A Thousand and One Nights*.

The spectacle provoked in turn perplexity, laughter, amazement, and disapproval.

Nicole and Béatrice always uttered cries of delight when they saw their little sister. Some mothers said in loud and audible voices, "No child should be dressed up like that!"

"She isn't a circus animal."

"I wouldn't be surprised if that child turned out badly."

"It's shocking, using children to draw attention to yourself like that."

There were also adults whose hearts melted at the

apparition. The apparition took pleasure in their admiring looks, for she had noticed, in the mirror, that she was very beautiful—and had felt a voluptuous excitement as a result.

Here we should digress in order to conclude an incipient sidetrack that has already gone on too long. We might call it the "Arsinoé encyclical."

In Molière's play *The Misanthrope,* the young, pretty, and flirtatious Célimène finds herself being scolded by a bitter old hag named Arsinoé who, green with jealousy, comes to tell her that she should not enjoy her beauty so much. Célimène offers her an utterly delectable reply, concluding "you would do well to concern yourself less with the actions of others, and take a little more pains with your own." Alas, Molière's genius seems to have counted for nothing, since now, almost four centuries later, people persist in delivering moralistic, wet-blanket obloquies when anyone has the temerity to smile at her own reflection.

The author of these lines has never felt any pleasure at seeing herself in a mirror, but had such grace been bestowed upon her, she would not have refused herself that innocent pleasure.

The following is addressed particularly to all the Arsinoés in the world. Who are these fortunate creatures hurting by enjoying their own beauty? Are they not rather alleviating our sad condition, by allowing us to gaze upon such marvelous faces?

Here the author is talking not about those who have transformed fake prettiness into contempt and exclusiveness, but those who, simply delighted by their own image, wish to bind others to their natural joy.

If these Arsinoés used the same energy trying to get the best out of their own physiques as they do ranting at girls like Célimène, they would be only half as ugly as they are.

BY THE END of school, Arsinoés of all ages were furious with Plectrude. Good Célimène that she was, she didn't care, and paid attention only to her admirers, on whose faces she could read enchanted surprise. She took an innocent pleasure in this, which made her even more beautiful.

Clémence brought the three children back home. As the older girls did their homework or a little drawing, she prepared proper meals—ham, mashed potato— sometimes smiling when she thought about the different kinds of food she gave her various offspring.

But she could not have been accused of favoritism: she loved all three children equally. Each one was loved in the image of what inspired it: well-behaved and solid for Nicole and Béatrice, wild and enchanted for Plectrude. It didn't make her any less of a good mother.

WHEN THE LITTLE one was asked what she wanted for her fourth birthday, she replied without a moment's hesitation: "Ballet shoes."

This was a subtle way of informing her parents what she wanted to be when she grew up. Nothing could have given Clémence greater pleasure: at the age of fifteen she had failed the entrance exam for the *petits rats*—"little rats"—of the Paris Opéra School, and had never got over it.

Plectrude was enrolled in a course of ballet lessons for four-year-olds. Not only was she not rejected because of her hard stare, she was immediately distinguished by it.

"This little girl has the eyes of a dancer," said the ballet teacher.

"How can anyone have the eyes of a dancer?" asked Clémence, astonished. "Wouldn't you say that she has a dancer's body, a dancer's grace?"

"She has all that. But she also has a dancer's eyes, and, believe me, it's the most important and most precious thing. If a ballerina has no gaze, she will never be present in her own dance."

What was certain was that, when she danced, Plectrude's eyes attained an extraordinary intensity. *She's found herself,* thought Clémence.

THOUGH NOW FIVE, the little girl was still not going to nursery school. Her mother felt that going to ballet classes four times a week was enough to teach her the art of getting along with other children.

"They teach other things than that in nursery school," Denis protested.

"Does she really need to know how to stick stickers, and make pasta necklaces, and macramé?" said his wife, staring at the ceiling.

In fact Clémence wanted to prolong her secret life with Plectrude for as long as she possibly could. She adored the days she spent in her daughter's company. And the dance lessons had one undeniable superiority over nursery school: the mother was allowed to be present.

She watched ecstatic with pride. The other little girls looked like ducklings.

After class, the teacher made a point of coming to tell her, "She's got to stay at it. She's quite exceptional."

Clémence brought her daughter home, repeating the compliments she had received about her. Plectrude accepted them with the grace of a diva.

"Anyway, nursery school isn't compulsory," Denis

concluded, with a certain amused fatalism typical of the submissive husband.

BUT—ALAS!—KINDERGARTEN *was* compulsory.

In August, as her husband was preparing to put Plectrude's name down for it, Clémence protested. "She's only five years old!"

"She'll be six in October."

This time he stuck to his guns. On the first of September not two but three children were driven to school.

Plectrude was not opposed to the idea. She liked showing off her satchel. So there were strange scenes as Plectrude set off for her new school: it was the mother, not her child, who wept.

Plectrude was soon disenchanted with kindergarten. It was very different from ballet lessons. You had to stay sitting down without moving for hours. You had to listen to a woman who wasn't saying anything interesting.

Recess came. She dashed into the playground to practice her jetés. Her poor legs had been still for too long.

While she did this the other children played together. Most of them had known each other since nursery school. They told each other things. Plec-

28

trude wondered what they could have to tell each other.

She went closer to listen. She heard a steady hum produced by a large number of voices, not all of which she could match with their owners. They were talking about the teacher, holidays, someone called Magali, and playing Chinese jumping rope. *Give me a chocolate bar,* and *Magali's my friend, shut up you're too stupid, aaaaaoooww, haven't you got any Snickers, why aren't I in Magali's class, stop it, we're not going to play with you, I'm going to tell teacher, Ooh you sneak, all you had to do was stop pushing me, Magali likes me more than you, and anyway your shoes are ugly, stop it, girls are so stupid, I'm glad I'm not in your class, Magali . . .*

Plectrude ran off, terrified.

THEN YOU HAD to listen to the teacher again. What she said wasn't always interesting but, at least, it was about one thing rather than all that chatter. It would have been bearable if she didn't have to remain immobile. Fortunately there was a window.

"You there!"

At the fifth "You there!"—and by virtue of the fact that the whole class was laughing—Plectrude realized that she was being addressed, and turned with startled eyes.

29

"Well it's about time!" said the teacher.

All the children were staring at the girl who had been singled out. It was an awful feeling. She wondered what her crime could possibly be.

"You will look at me, not the window!" said the woman.

As there was no possible response to this, the child said nothing.

"You say, 'Yes, miss!' "

"Yes, miss."

"What's your name?" the teacher asked, as though she was thinking, *I've got my eye on you!*

"Plectrude."

"I'm sorry?"

" 'Plectrude,' " she articulated in a clear voice.

The children were still too little to be aware of the outrageousness of the name. The teacher opened her eyes wide, checked her class list, and finally said, "Well, if you're trying to attract attention, you've succeeded," as though Plectrude had chosen her own first name.

The girl thought, *She's the one who's been trying to attract attention all morning. You can tell she can't bear not to be looked at. She wants to be noticed, but she's not in the slightest bit interesting.*

But the teacher was the boss and the child obeyed. She began staring at her with her eyes wide open. Miss was disconcerted, but said nothing. The worst thing happened at lunchtime. The pupils were led into a vast cafeteria dominated by the smell of children's vomit and disinfectant.

They had to sit down at tables of ten. Plectrude didn't know where to go and closed her eyes to avoid having to choose. She found herself at a steam table staffed by large women.

Others carried food containers whose contents were unidentifiable. Panicking, Plectrude could not decide which foreign bodies to put onto her plate. So the ladies served her themselves, and she found herself looking at a dish of greenish mush and little squares of brown meat.

She wondered what she had done to deserve this. Until then, as far as she was concerned, lunch had been a pure enchantment: by candlelight, protected from the world by red velvet drapes, a beautiful mother, magnificently dressed, bringing her cakes and creams that she didn't even have to eat, all to the sound of heavenly music. And now, amid the cries of hideous, dirty children, in an ugly, foul-smelling hall, they slopped green mush onto her plate, and told her she couldn't leave the cafeteria until she swallowed everything.

Outraged by the injustices of fate, the child started eating. It was horrible. She had trouble swallowing.

Halfway through, she vomited onto her plate and understood the source of the smell.

"Yuck, you're disgusting!" the other children said to her.

A lady came to take her plate away. "Oh, my goodness!"

At least she wasn't forced to eat anything else that day.

AFTER THIS NIGHTMARE she had to listen once again to the woman who was trying, without success, to make herself interesting. On the blackboard, the teacher jotted down combinations of letters that weren't even pretty to look at. Finally, at half past four, Plectrude was allowed to leave this absurd and abject place. Outside, she spotted her mother, and ran toward her as one runs toward a safe haven.

Clémence had only to look at her to know how much her child had suffered. She swept her up in her arms. "Now, now, it's over, it's over."

"Really? I won't be going back?" asked the little girl hopefully.

"Yes, you will. It's required. But you'll get used to it."

Now Plectrude understood that we aren't put on this planet to enjoy ourselves.

. . .

SHE DIDN'T GET used to it. School was hell.

Luckily, there were the ballet lessons. What her schoolteacher taught was useless and stupid. What her dance teacher taught was precious and sublime.

This discrepancy began to create some problems. After a few months, most of the other children in her class were able to decipher letters and draw their shapes. Plectrude had decided such matters had nothing to do with her: when her time came, and the teacher showed her a letter written on the board, she pronounced the first sound that came into her head, always completely wrong, making her lack of progress a little too obvious.

The teacher called in her parents. Denis was embarrassed. Nicole and Béatrice were good pupils, and he was not accustomed to this kind of humiliation. Although she would not have admitted it, Clémence felt a vague kind of pride. Her little rebel didn't do anything the way anyone else did.

"If it goes on like this, she's going to be held back a year," the teacher told them ominously.

Plectrude's mother widened her eyes. She had never heard of a child having to repeat kindergarten. It struck her as daring and high-minded for its sheer insolence.

What child would dare to repeat kindergarten, where even the most mediocre pupils get through without too much difficulty? Her daughter was already proudly asserting her independence—no, her exceptional nature.

That wasn't how Denis saw it. "We'll work this out!" he told the teacher. "We'll take charge of things!"

"Is there any chance of her not repeating a year?" asked Clémence, filled with a wondrous hope that the others misinterpreted.

"Certainly. If she can learn to read her letters before the end of the school year."

Plectrude's mother concealed her disappointment. It had been too lovely to be true.

"She will learn to read them," said Denis firmly. "You know, it's strange. The child seems very bright."

"That's entirely possible. The problem is that she isn't interested."

She isn't interested! thought Clémence. *She's amazing! She isn't interested! Other kids swallow the lot without a murmur. But my Plectrude has already decided what's worthwhile and what isn't!*

"I'M NOT INTERESTED in it, Daddy."

"Come on, of course learning to read is interesting!" Denis protested.

"Why?"

"So that you can read stories."

"The teacher sometimes reads us stories from our reading book. They're so annoying that I stop listening after two minutes."

Clémence mentally applauded.

"Do you want to take kindergarten over? Is that what you want?" asked Denis, furious.

"I want to be a dancer."

"To be a dancer, you've got to get through kindergarten."

Clémence suddenly realized that her husband was right. She immediately went and got a gigantic nineteenth-century book from her bedroom.

She took the child on her knees and went through the entire collection of fairy tales with her, being careful not to read them, only to point out the lovely illustrations.

The child had never felt such wonder as when she discovered princesses too magnificent to touch the ground with their feet, or locked up in towers, or who talked to bluebirds that were really princes, or who disguised themselves as scullery maids only to reappear even more ravishing than before four pages later.

At that moment she knew, with that certainty only little girls are capable of, that one day she would be one of those creatures who transform toads, defeat witches, and dazzle princes.

"Don't worry," Clémence told her husband. "She'll be reading by the end of the week."

THE TRUTH EXCEEDED her prediction: two days later, Plectrude's brain had turned to its own advantage the boring and pointless letters it didn't realize it had absorbed during school, and found a coherence between signs, sounds, and meaning. Two days later, she was reading a hundred times better than the best pupils. There is only one key to knowledge, and that is desire.

She had looked on the fairy-tale book as an instruction manual to help her become one of the princesses in the illustrations. Because reading was necessary to her now, her intelligence had grasped it.

"Why didn't you show her that book before?" Denis cried in delight.

"I didn't want to spoil it by showing it to her too soon. She had to be old enough to appreciate a work of art."

THUS, TWO DAYS after her meeting with Plectrude's parents, the teacher was astounded to find that the little dunce who had not been able to identify a single letter of the alphabet was now reading like the best of the ten-year-olds.

In forty-eight hours, the child had learned what a professional hadn't managed to teach her in five months. The teacher thought her parents must have a secret method, and called them to find out what it was. Denis, full of pride, told her the truth: "We didn't do anything at all. We just showed her a book that was so beautiful it made her want to read. That's what was missing."

Plectrude's father didn't realize that he was making a dreadful blunder.

The teacher, who had never much cared for Plectrude, now began to despise her. Not only did she consider this miracle a personal humiliation, she also felt for the little girl all the malice a mediocre mind feels for a superior one: "Little Miss Princess needed a beautiful book! How about this one! It's beautiful enough for everyone else!"

Perplexed and furious, she read from cover to cover the book that was under attack for being uninteresting. It told of the daily life of Thierry, a smiling little boy, and his big sister, Micheline, who made him bread and jam for his afternoon snack, and kept him out of trouble because she was sensible.

But it's charming! she exclaimed to herself as she finished reading. *It's fresh, it's delightful. What else could the silly goose possibly need?*

What she needed was gold, myrrh, and frankincense, mauve and lilies, midnight blue velvet scattered with stars, engravings by Gustave Doré, unsmiling little girls with lovely, serious eyes, gloomily seductive wolves, evil forests—she needed all kinds of things. Not Thierry and his big sister, Micheline.

FROM THEN ON the teacher never missed an opportunity to voice her disgust with Plectrude. Because she was at the bottom of the class in arithmetic, the teacher called her "hopeless." One day when Plectrude wasn't able to perform even the simplest of additions on the blackboard, Miss told her to return to her seat, saying, "You might as well stop trying. You'll never be able to do it."

The other pupils were still at that follow-the-leader age at which the adult is always right, and dissent unthinkable. So Plectrude was the object of universal contempt.

In her ballet classes, by the same logic, she was the queen. The teacher was ecstatic about her gifts, and, without daring to say so (because it was not a very good pedagogic approach), treated her as the best student she had ever had. The other little girls worshiped Plectrude and jostled one another to dance next to her.

As a result she led two quite distinct lives. There was school life, where it was Plectrude versus everyone else, and life in her ballet class, where she was the star.

She was clear-sighted enough to know that the children in her dance class would be the first to despise her if they were in school with her. For that reason, Plectrude was distant toward the girls who sought her friendship—and this intensified their passion for her.

PLECTRUDE ONLY JUST passed kindergarten by making sustained efforts at arithmetic. As a reward, her parents gave her a barre so that she could practice her exercises at home. She spent the summer training. By the end of August she could hold her foot in her hand and extend her leg.

When she returned to school, a surprise was waiting for her: the class's makeup was the same as it had been the previous year, but with one important exception. There was a new girl.

Roselyne was a stranger to everyone except Plectrude, because she was in her ballet class. Struck dumb with happiness to be in her idol's class, she asked permission to sit next to Plectrude. Never before had anyone asked to sit there. The request was granted.

As far as Roselyne was concerned, Plectrude represented the absolute ideal. She spent hours studying this inaccessible muse who had miraculously become her neighbor at school.

Plectrude wondered whether the worship would survive discovery of her being unpopular in the classroom. One day, when the teacher was remarking upon her weakness at arithmetic, the children ventured some snide comments about their fellow pupil. Roselyne flew into a rage at their behavior. "Have you seen how they treat you?"

Plectrude, who was used to it, shrugged her shoulders. Roselyne only admired her all the more.

"I hate them!" she said.

Plectrude then knew that she had a friend. This changed her life.

How can one explain what friendship means to children? They believe that it is the duty of their family to love them. It never occurs to them to see value in something that is, as far as they are concerned, merely part of the job. Most children say, "I love him because he is my brother (my father, my sister . . .). I have to."

The friend is the one who chooses her. The friend is the one who gives her what is not her due. Friendship is the supreme luxury—and luxury is what noble souls desire most ardently. Friendship gives the child some sense of the splendor of life.

Returning home, Plectrude solemnly announced, "I've got a friend."

It was the first time she had said it. Immediately Clémence felt a twinge of jealousy in her heart. However, she very quickly managed to reason that there would never be any competition between this outsider and herself. Friends move on. Mothers don't.

"Invite her over for dinner," she said to her daughter.

Plectrude opened her eyes wide with terror.

"Why?"

"What do you mean, why? We want to meet your friend."

This was how the little girl discovered that when you wanted to meet someone, you invited them over for dinner. It struck her as disturbing and absurd. Did you know people any better once you'd seen them eating? She imagined what they thought of her at school, where the cafeteria was a den of torture and vomit.

If *she* wanted to know someone, she would invite her over to play. People revealed themselves at play.

NEVERTHELESS, ROSELYNE WAS invited over for dinner, because that was the way adults did things. Every-

thing went very well. Plectrude waited impatiently for
the small talk to come to an end. She knew her friend
would sleep in her bedroom, and that idea struck her as
marvelous.

Darkness, finally.

"Are you afraid of the dark?" she asked hopefully.

"Yes," said Roselyne.

"I'm not!"

"I see monsters in the dark."

"So do I. But I like that."

"You like dragons?"

"Yes! And bats."

"Don't they frighten you?"

"No. Because I'm their queen."

"How do you know?"

"I decided."

Roselyne thought this an admirable explanation.

"I'm the queen of everything you see in the dark:
jellyfish, crocodiles, snakes, spiders, sharks, dinosaurs,
slugs, octopuses."

"Don't they disgust you?"

"No. I think they're lovely."

"Doesn't anything disgust you?"

"Dried figs."

"Dried figs aren't disgusting!"

"Have you eaten them?"

"Yes."

"Well don't, not if you love me."

"Why not?"

"People who sell them chew them and then put them back in the packet."

"What?"

"Why do you think they're all mushy and horrible?"

"Is that true?"

"I swear. People chew them up and then spit them back out again."

"Yuck!"

"There's nothing in the world more disgusting than dried figs."

They swooned with a shared revulsion that drove them to ecstasy. They endlessly detailed the repugnant aspects of this desiccated fruit, uttering cries of pleasure.

"I'm never going to eat them ever again," Roselyne said solemnly.

"Even under torture?"

"Even under torture!"

"And what if someone stuffs them into your mouth by force?"

"I swear I'll throw up!" the child declared, with the conviction of a young bride.

That night elevated their friendship to the level of a secret cult.

. . .

PLECTRUDE'S STATUS HAD changed in school. She had moved from pestiferous outcast to adulated best friend. Had she been adored by a clod, she could have gone on being undesirable. But in the eyes of the pupils, Roselyne could do no wrong. Her sole defect, which consisted of being a new girl, was but a very temporary stain on her character. They began to wonder if they hadn't been mistaken about Plectrude.

Of course, no discussions about this actually took place. The thoughts circulated in the collective unconscious of the class. Their impact was all the greater for it.

Certainly, Plectrude remained a dunce in arithmetic and many other areas. But the children discovered that a weakness in certain subjects, particularly when it was taken to extremes, could sometimes have something admirable and heroic about it. Gradually they came to understand the charm of subversion.

The teacher didn't.

PLECTRUDE'S PARENTS WERE again summoned.

"With your permission, we are going to have your child undergo some tests."

Denis felt profoundly humiliated. They were saying

his daughter was deficient. Clémence was delighted: Plectrude was extraordinary. Even if they detected a mental defect, she would take it as a sign that her child was one of the elect.

So Plectrude was subjected to all kinds of logical sequences, abstruse lists, geometrical figures containing irrelevant puzzles, formulae pompously called algorithms. She replied mechanically, as quickly as possible, in order to hide a violent to desire to laugh.

Was it chance or the brilliance of instinct? She did so well that everyone was astonished. And thus it was that within the space of an hour, Plectrude went from class dunce to genius.

"I am not surprised," her mother commented, vexed at her husband's amazement.

THE CHANGE OF TERMINOLOGY conferred advantages, as the child soon became aware. Previously, when she couldn't work out a problem, the teacher would give her a pained look, and the more hateful pupils laughed. Now, when she couldn't get to the end of a simple task, the teacher contemplated her like the albatross in Baudelaire's poem: her massive intelligence prevented her from doing basic adding and subtracting. Her fellow pupils were ashamed at having so stupidly reached a solution.

Given that she really was intelligent, she wondered why she couldn't solve easy math questions. During the tests, she had given correct answers to exercises that were actually far harder.

She remembered that she had not been thinking at all during those tests, and concluded from this that the key to everything was absolute thoughtlessness.

From that point onward, Plectrude took care not to think when solving a task and instead wrote down the first numbers that came into her head. The results weren't any better, but they weren't any worse, either. Consequently she decided to keep to this method, which, by virtue of being just as ineffective as the earlier one, was fantastically liberating. And that was how she became the most highly esteemed dunce in France.

It would all have been perfect had there not, at the end of each school year, been annoying formalities designed to select those who would be lucky enough to move up to the next class.

This was a nightmarish period for Plectrude, who was only too well aware of the role chance played in these events. Fortunately, her reputation as a genius preceded her: when the teacher saw her results in mathematics, he concluded that the child's answers might be right in another dimension, and ignored the scores. Or else he questioned the little girl about her reasoning, and what she said left him flabbergasted. She had, you see, learned to mimic what people thought was the language of a gifted girl. For example, at the end of a stream of utter gibberish, she would conclude with a limpid "It's obvious."

It wasn't obvious at all to her teachers. But they preferred not to advertise this fact, and always gave their student their blessing to move on.

GENIUS OR DUNCE, the little girl had only one obsession: dancing.

The more she grew, the more amazed the teachers were by her gifts. She had virtuosity and grace, rigor and imagination, prettiness and a sense of the tragic, precision and spirit.

The best thing was that it was impossible not to see that she was happy dancing—prodigiously happy. You could feel her delight at handing her body over to dance. It was as though her soul had waited ten thousand years to do just that. Arabesques freed her from some mysterious inner conflict.

She had a sense for the theatrical: the presence of an audience highlighted her talent, and the keener the focus upon her, the more intense her performance.

There was also the miracle of her slenderness. Plectrude was, and would remain, as thin as a figure in an

47

Egyptian relief. Her weightlessness defied the laws of gravity.

Finally, without consulting one another, her teachers all said the same thing about her: "She has the eyes of a dancer."

CLÉMENCE SOMETIMES HAD the feeling that too many fairies had leaned over the child's cradle. She worried that Plectrude would attract the thunderbolts of the gods.

Fortunately, her other daughters accommodated themselves to the miracle without great difficulty. Plectrude had not encroached upon the territories of her two older sisters. Nicole was top of the class in science and physical education, Béatrice had a flair for math and a knack for history. Perhaps out of an instinctive sense of diplomacy, Plectrude was hopeless in all these subjects—even in gymnastics, for which her dancing seemed to be of no help to her.

So Denis assigned access to a third of the universe to each of his children. "Nicole is going to be a scientist and an athlete, maybe an astronaut. Béatrice will be an intellectual; her head crammed with numbers and facts, she'll analyze historical events. And Plectrude is an artist brimming over with charisma; she'll be a dancer or a politician, or both at once."

He concluded by laughing loudly, from pride rather than doubt. The children enjoyed listening to him, because his words were flattering, though the youngest couldn't help feeling slightly perplexed, both at these predictions which struck her as vacuous and at the assurance with which her father made them.

Despite being only ten years old, and not advanced for her age, Plectrude had nonetheless learned one important thing: that people on this earth did not receive what was their due.

BUT BEING TEN YEARS old is the best thing that can happen to a human being. Especially to a little dancer in full command of her art.

Ten is the most sunlit moment of growing up. No sign of adolescence is yet visible on the horizon: nothing but mature childhood, already rich in experience, unburdened by that feeling of loss that assaults you from the first hint of puberty onward. At ten, you aren't necessarily happy, but you are certainly alive, more alive than anyone else.

Plectrude was a knot of the most intense vitality. She was at the summit of her reign over her dancing school, of which she was the uncontested queen. She ruled over her class, which threatened to turn into a dunceocracy in which the one most useless at math, science, history, and geography was the undisputed genius.

She ruled over the heart of her mother, who nurtured an infinite passion for her. And she ruled over Roselyne, whose love for Plectrude matched her admiration.

However, Plectrude's extraordinary status did not turn her into one of those stuck-up ten-year-old madams who think they are above the laws of friendship. She was devoted to Roselyne and worshiped her friend every bit as much as her Roselyne worshiped her.

Some obscure prescience seemed to warn her that she might topple from her throne. She remembered when she had been the laughingstock of the class.

ROSELYNE AND PLECTRUDE had already gotten married several times, most often to each other. On some occasions they also married a boy from their class who, in the most fabulous of ceremonies, was represented sometimes in effigy, sometimes by Roselyne or Plectrude disguised as a man—a top hat did the trick.

The husband's identity, in fact, was of little importance. So long as he displayed no unacceptable vices (piggishness, a squeaky voice, or a propensity to begin his sentences with, "Know what? . . ."), he was suitable. The purpose of the game was to create a nuptial dance, a kind of dance-play worthy of neoclassical drama, with songs whose lyrics were as tragic as humanly possible.

Inevitably, after all too brief a marriage, the husband got turned into a bird or a toad, and the wife locked up once more in a high tower with some impossible task to perform.

"Why is the ending always so sad?" Roselyne asked one day.

"Because it's much nicer that way," Plectrude assured her.

THAT WINTER, PLECTRUDE invented a sublimely heroic game. It involved allowing yourself to be buried in snow, not moving, and not putting up the slightest resistance.

"Making a snowman is too easy," she had decreed. "You have to *become* a snowman, or else lie down in a garden under the snow."

Roselyne looked at her with skeptical admiration.

"You be the snowman and I'll be the one who lies down," Plectrude went on.

Her friend didn't dare voice her qualms. The two girls found themselves beneath the snow, one lying on the ground, the other standing up. The one standing up soon ceased to see the fun in all this. Her feet were cold, she wanted to move, she had no desire to become a living monument. On top of that she was bored because, apart from being statues, the two little girls had agreed to remain silent.

The recumbent figure was exultant. It had kept its eyes open, as corpses do before others intervene. It had relinquished its body, parting company with the sensation of freezing, and from the physical fear of leaving its skin. All that remained was a face open to the forces of the sky.

Plectrude's girlish ten-year-old frame was not present, not that it would have been much of a burden. The recumbent figure had preserved only the very minimum of itself, in order to put up as little resistance as possible to the pale curtain of snowflakes.

Eyes wide-open contemplated the most fascinating spectacle in the world: descending white death, sent down by the universe as a piece of a jigsaw puzzle, of some single vast mystery.

Sometimes the eyes studied the body, which was covered before the face was, because the clothes acted as insulation. Then the eyes returned to the clouds again, and gradually the warmth faded from the cheeks, and soon the shroud was complete and the recumbent figure stopped smiling so as not to spoil its elegance.

. . .

A BILLION SNOWFLAKES later, the thin silhouette of
the recumbent figure was already almost indis-
cernible, barely a lump in the white amalgam of the
garden.

The only cheating lay in its blinking from time to
time, sometimes reflexively. This meant that the eyes
had retained their access to the sky, and were still able
to observe the slow, deadly cascade.

Air passed through the layer of ice that now envel-
oped the figure, so it did not suffocate. It was engag-
ed in a tremendous, superhuman struggle with some
unknown force, some unidentifiable angel—was it
with the snow, or with the recumbent figure?—but
also felt a serenity that came of the most profound
acceptance.

AS FAR AS THE SNOWMAN was concerned, on the
other hand, things weren't quite so peachy. Undisci-
plined, and unconvinced of the pertinence of the experiment, it couldn't stop moving. Besides, the upright
posture was less conducive to burial and even less to
submission.

Roselyne looked at the recumbent figure, wondering what she should do. She knew her friend was the kind to take things to their conclusion, and knew that she would forbid her to intervene on her behalf.

She had been instructed to remain silent, but decided to be disobedient: "Plectrude, can you hear me?"

There was no reply.

It was probable that Plectrude, in her fury at the snowman's interference, had decided to punish him with silence. Such would have been entirely in line with her character.

But it could also mean something very different.

A storm raged in Roselyne's skull.

THE SNOW LAY SO thick on the face of the recumbent figure that it wouldn't be shaken off, even by blinking. The eyes were closed over.

At first, daylight had still managed to pass through the veil, and the figure had the sublime vision of a dome of crystals a few millimeters away from its pupils, lovely as a trove of gemstones.

Now the shroud had grown opaque. The figure found itself in darkness and the darkness was fascinating: how incredible that such darkness reigned beneath such whiteness.

The amalgam was increasingly dense. The recumbent figure noted that air no longer filtered through. It wanted to get up, to free itself of its gag, but the layer of ice was frozen solid, forming an igloo in the exact proportions of its body, and it now knew that it was imprisoned. This would be its tomb.

Then the living behaved like the living: it screamed. Its cries were muffled by the snow. All that emerged was a barely audible moan. Finally, Roselyne heard the sound, and hurled herself on her friend, dragging her from beneath her snowflake tomb, using her hands like a mechanical digger. The girl's blue face appeared, spectral in its beauty.

"It was magnificent!"

"Why didn't you get up? You were dying!"

"Because I was trapped. The snow had frozen."

"No it hadn't! I was able to pull you out with my hands!"

"Really? Then the cold must have made me too weak to move."

She said this in such an offhand manner that Roselyne, perplexed, wondered whether she was pretending. But her friend really was blue. And you can't pretend to die.

Plectrude stood up and looked at the sky.

"What just happened to me was fantastic!"

"You're crazy. I don't know if you realize that you wouldn't be alive without me."

"Yes, you've saved my life. That makes everything even more beautiful."

"What's so beautiful about it?"

"Everything!"

The elated girl went home and suffered only a bad cold.

Roselyne thought she had gotten off lightly. Her admiration for Plectrude didn't stop Roselyne from thinking her friend was losing her marbles. She always had to be center stage, she had to surround herself with grandeur, to seek out dangers where there were none, and then to miraculously emerge from them.

Roselyne could never shake off her suspicion that Plectrude had remained trapped beneath her snowy shroud on purpose. She knew her friend would have thought the whole story much less heroic if she had gotten out by herself. She had chosen to wait to be saved to conform to her aesthetic values. Plectrude might even have been capable of allowing herself to die rather than bend the heroic rules her character imposed upon her.

Yet Roselyne could never confirm any of this. Sometimes she even thought the opposite was true: *After all, she did call me for help. If she had really been insane, she wouldn't have done that.*

But other troubling things happened. Intriguing things. When they were waiting together for the bus, Plectrude would often stand in the road and stay there even when cars came toward her. Roselyne would tug her bossily back onto the sidewalk, then see that her friend's face had an utterly rapturous expression.

That annoyed her a little.

One day, she resolved not to intervene, just to see.

A truck was heading straight for Plectrude. She must have known it was coming, yet she didn't move. Roselyne realized that her friend was gazing straight into her eyes. *I won't save her, I won't save her,* she kept repeating.

The truck was getting dangerously close and blowing its horn.

"Look out!" yelled Roselyne.

Plectrude stood motionless, staring into her friend's eyes.

At the very last second, Roselyne furiously grabbed her by the arm and dragged her out of the road.

Plectrude's mouth was contorted with delight.

"You saved me," she said with a sigh of ecstasy.

"You're completely crazy! That truck could have crushed us both. Would you have wanted me to die for you?"

"No," Plectrude replied, astonished, apparently never having considered that possibility.

"So never do it again!"

PLECTRUDE RAN THROUGH the scene in the snow a thousand times in her own mind.

Her version was very different from Roselyne's.

She was so much the dancer that she lived out every last scene of her life as though it were in a ballet. Her choreographies were designed for tragedy to appear at every turn: what would have been weird in everyday life wasn't weird on stage, particularly in a dance.

I gave myself to the snow in the garden. I lay down and it built a cathedral around me. I saw it slowly raising the walls, then the vaults. I was the recumbent figure, with the whole cathedral all to myself. Then the doors closed and death came in search of me, white and gentle at first, then black and violent. It was going to take me away but my guardian angel saved me at the very last second.

It was best if being saved happened at the very last second. Anything less would have been a failure of taste.

Roselyne didn't know she was playing the part of guardian angel.

PLECTRUDE TURNED TWELVE. It was the first time that a birthday had given her a vague twinge in the heart. Another year had always seemed like a good thing, a proud heroic step toward a future that was bound to be beautiful. Twelve was like a boundary: the last innocent birthday.

She refused to even think about thirteen. The world of teenagers left her cold. Thirteen was sure to be full of breakups, illness, gloom, acne, first periods, bras, and other horrors.

Twelve was the last birthday when she could feel sheltered from the calamities of adolescence. With delight she stroked her flat torso.

The dancer went and snuggled in her mother's arms. Her mother happily fussed over her, cosseted her, said loving little words to her, rubbed her back and her arms—lavishing on her that ecstatic affection that the very best mothers give to their daughters.

Plectrude closed her eyes with pleasure. No love could give her as much satisfaction as her mother's did. The idea of being in a boy's arms didn't fire her imagination. Being in the arms of Clémence was the absolute. Would her mother still love her as much when she was a pimply adolescent? The idea terrified her. She didn't dare ask.

FROM THAT POINT ON, Plectrude cultivated her childhood. She was like a landowner who had an enormous

59

estate at his disposal for many years but, following some disaster, was left with only a little plot. Making a virtue of a necessity, she lavished care upon her patch of land, pampering those flowers of childhood that still survived.

She wore her hair in braids or pigtails, she dressed only in jeans, she walked around clutching a teddy bear, and sat on the ground to lace up her boots.

She didn't have to pretend to behave like a child; she just drifted to the side of herself that she liked best, aware that she wouldn't be able to do so much longer.

Such rules might seem strange, but they aren't strange to pre-teen children, who minutely observe which of their playmates are moving ahead and which are lagging behind. Their admiration is as paradoxical as their contempt. Those who play up either their precocity or their late development earn opprobrium, punishment, and ridicule, or, though far more rarely, a heroic reputation.

Ask any girl in the seventh or eighth grade which of her classmates are already wearing bras and you will be astonished by the exactitude of the reply.

In Plectrude's class—she was already in the eighth grade—there were some who mocked her pigtails, but these were the girls who were advanced in terms of bra-wearing, which brought them more teasing than praise, and their mockery was a form of compensation for their jealousy over the dancer's flat torso.

As for the boys, their attitude toward the bra-wearers was ambiguous: they ogled them and at the same time said horrible things about them. That, incidentally, is a habit that the members of the male sex keep throughout their lives. They make a point of slandering the very things that haunt their masturbatory obsessions.

The first manifestations of sexuality were appearing on the horizon. Plectrude saw that she must arm herself with an emphatic form of innocence. She could not put her fear into words. She knew only that if some of her classmates were already prepared for strange things, she was not. Unconsciously she began warning the others of this, by forcefully reinforcing her childhood state.

IN NOVEMBER, A NEW arrival was announced.

Plectrude liked new pupils. Would Roselyne have become her best friend if she hadn't been a new girl, five years before? The little dancer was forever linking up with strangers, to their varying degrees of alarm.

Most of the children showed no mercy toward the newcomer: the slightest differences (peeling an orange with a knife, or saying "crap!" instead of "shit!") provoked whoops of derision.

Plectrude was delighted by odd behavior. She felt the enthusiasm an ethnologist feels when being introduced to the customs of an exotic tribe. ("The way he peels his orange is amazing!" or, "Saying 'crap' is very cool!") She greeted newcomers like a Tahitian welcoming European sailors, brandishing her smile rather than a garland of hibiscus flowers.

The arrival of a new pupil was particularly poignant when it happened in the middle of the school year instead of September.

This was the case with the new boy. The little dancer was already extremely well disposed toward him by the time he walked into the classroom. Plectrude's face froze in a mixture of horror and admiration.

His name was Mathieu Saladin. He found a seat at the back, near the radiator.

Plectrude didn't hear a word the teacher said. She was feeling something extraordinary. She had a pain in her chest, and she loved it. She kept wanting to turn around to look at the boy. Usually she gawked at people to the point of rudeness. This time she couldn't.

At last it was recess. Ordinarily, the little dancer would have walked up to the new boy with a luminous smile. This time she remained desperately motionless.

The other kids, however, kept to their hostile habits.
"So this new guy, did he fight in Vietnam or what?"
"Let's call him Scarface."

Plectrude felt anger welling up in her. It was all she could do not to yell, "Shut up! It's a wonderful scar! I've never seen anyone so handsome!"

Mathieu Saladin's mouth was split by a long perpendicular scar, well stitched, but visible. It was much too long to suggest the post-operation mark of a harelip.

She knew it was a fencing scar. The boy's last name evoked the stories of *A Thousand and One Nights*, and, in fact, Plectrude was not mistaken in this, for Mathieu Saladin's name was of distant Persian origin. Henceforth it went without saying that the boy possessed a scimitar. He must have used it to carve up some evil Crusader who had come to claim the tomb of Christ. Before biting the dust, the Crusader, in a gesture of revolting pettiness (because cutting someone into pieces was considered perfectly normal at the time), had thrown his sword right into his mouth, forever inscribing their battle upon his face.

The new boy's face had otherwise regular, classic features, pleasant and impassive. This made his scar stand out all the more. Plectrude marveled in silence at what she was feeling.

"So are you going to welcome the new boy the way you usually do?" asked Roselyne.

The dancer worried that her silence risked attracting attention. She summoned her courage, took a deep breath, and walked toward the boy, smiling tensely.

At that very moment he was with a big loud kid named Didier, who was repeating a year. Didier was trying to impress Mathieu Saladin by boasting that he had a distant cousin with a scarred face.

"Hello, Mathieu," she mumbled. "My name is Plectrude."

"Hello," he replied, politely.

Normally, she would have added something kind along the lines of: "Welcome to our school," or, "I hope you'll be happy here." Now she couldn't say a word. She turned and went back to her seat.

"A funny name, but a very pretty girl," commented Mathieu Saladin.

"Yeah, whatever," murmured Didier, acting blasé. "She's just a little kid. If you like chicks, come over here and take a look at Muriel. I call her 'melons.'"

"I can see why," replied Mathieu.

"Want to meet her?"

Before he even got a reply, Didier took Mathieu by the shoulder and led him up to the girl with the developing chest. Plectrude didn't hear what they were saying. She had a bitter taste in her mouth.

THE NIGHT AFTER THAT first encounter, Plectrude thought about her feelings for Mathieu.

He's for me. He's mine. He doesn't know it, but he belongs to me. Mathieu Saladin is for me. I don't care if it's in a month or twenty years. I swear it.

She repeated this to herself for hours, like an incantation, with a certainty that she would not feel again for a very long time.

The next day she had to face the facts: the new boy didn't so much as glance at her. She darted her marvelous eyes at him, but he didn't seem to notice.

"If he wasn't disfigured, he would be simply handsome. With that scar, he's magnificent," she said to herself.

Although she wasn't aware of it, her obsession with Mathieu's battle-scar was rich in meaning. Plectrude believed herself the real daughter of Clémence and Denis, and knew nothing of the circumstances of her birth, nor of the extraordinary violence that had accompanied it.

However there must have been some place within her that had soaked in murder and blood, because what she felt as she stared at Mathieu's scar was as deep as an ancestral wound.

ONE CONSOLATION WAS THAT if he was not interested in her, he didn't seem interested in anyone else either. Mathieu Saladin was even-tempered, and his face expressed a neutral politeness that applied equally to everyone. He was tall, very thin, and rather frail. His eyes shone with the wisdom of those who have suffered.

Whenever he was asked a question, he took time to reflect, and his response was always intelligent. Plectrude had never met a boy who was so far from being stupid.

He was neither especially good nor especially bad at any subject. He reached the level required, which meant that he didn't attract attention.

The little dancer, whose grades had not improved over the years, admired him for that. She had gained sympathy and a certain esteem among her peers. This was a good thing—otherwise she would have had even more trouble enduring the reactions that her answers provoked.

"What makes you say such nonsense?" some of her teachers asked, dismayed by the things Plectrude came up with.

She wanted to tell them she wasn't doing it on purpose, but had a feeling that would make things worse. If you made the whole class giggle, you might as well claim it was premeditated.

The teachers thought she was proud of the way the class reacted, and that she sought it on purpose. The opposite was the case. Whenever her gaffes provoked general hilarity, she wanted to sink into the floor.

An example: Once, when the class was discussing the city of Paris and its historical monuments, Plectrude was asked a question. The right answer was the Arc de Triomphe. The girl replied: "Joan of Arc's dad's house."

The class applauded this new piece of inanity with the enthusiasm an audience greets its favorite comedian.

Plectrude was at a loss. Her eyes sought out the face of Mathieu Saladin. She saw that he was laughing uncontrollably but without malice. She sighed, feeling a mixture of relief and contempt: relief, because things might have been worse; contempt, because his expression was very different from the one she had hoped to provoke in him.

If only he could see me dance! she thought.

Alas, how could she reveal her talent to him? There was no question of her going up to him and telling him point-blank that she was the star of her generation.

The worst of it was that he spent almost all his time with Didier. There was no reason this lout would tell him. Didier cared about as much about Plectrude as he did about the Treaty of Versailles. All he ever talked about was his stupid magazines, soccer, cigarettes, and beer. Being a year older than everyone else, he pretended to be grown up, claiming that he shaved—which was hard to believe—and bragging about his success with girls.

One might have wondered what Mathieu Saladin got out of hanging around with such a loser. It was clear that he didn't get anything out of it. He spent time with Didier because Didier was willing to spend time with him. One day she summoned up all her courage, and went to speak to her hero during recess. Her plan was to ask him who his favorite singer was.

He replied that he didn't especially like any particular singer, and that was why he had formed a band with a few friends.

"We meet in my parents' garage to make the kind of music that people would like to hear."

Plectrude almost fainted with admiration. She was too much in love to have the presence of mind to say: "I'd like to hear you and your group play."

She didn't say a word. From this Mathieu Saladin concluded that she wasn't interested; so he didn't invite her to come listen. Had he, she wouldn't have lost seven years of her life.

"What kind of music do you like?" he asked.

It was a disaster. She was still at the age when you listen to the same music your parents do. Denis and Clémence loved classic French chansons by singers like Barbara, Léo Ferré, Jacques Brel, Serge Reggiani, Charles Trenet. Still, if she had managed to mention one of those names, it would have been a respectable answer.

But Plectrude was ashamed of herself. *You're twelve years old and you don't even have tastes of your own. You aren't going to tell him that.*

She had no idea who the good singers were. She knew only a single name, and that was the one that she uttered:

"Dave."

Mathieu Saladin burst out laughing. *Man, but she's a strange one!* he thought.

She could have extricated herself from this situation, but she experienced it as a humiliation. She turned and left. *I'm never going to speak to him again.*

IT WAS THE START of a period of decline for Plectrude. Her grades, which had always been bad, started becoming execrable. Her reputation as a genius, which had kept her teachers guessing until then, was no longer enough.

She put her heart and soul into it; she chose educational suicide. As though intoxicated, she went crashing into the boundaries of incompetence and sent the pieces flying.

Her only choice, she felt, was to stop holding back. From now on she would let herself go, she would say whatever her inner dunce dictated—no more and no less. Her intention was not to attract attention (although, to be honest, she didn't mind that), but to be rejected, driven out, expelled like the foreign body that she was. Her answers to teachers' questions turned monstrous—by turns geographical ("the source of the Nile is in the Mediterranean and it doesn't flow into anything"), geometrical ("a right angle is ninety degrees Celsius"), grammatical ("the past participle agrees with women unless there's a man in the group"), historical ("Louis XIV became a Protestant when he married Edith of Nantes"), and biological ("cats have nubile eyes and nyctalopic claws")—and her classmates couldn't help feeling admiration.

Admiration that was, indeed, shared by the girl herself. In fact, it was with a degree of ecstatic astonishment that Plectrude heard herself coming up with such surrealistic pearls, and became aware of the infinitude of them within her.

The other students had come to the conclusion that Plectrude was doing this from pure provocation. Every time the teacher asked her a question, they held their breath, then marveled at the natural aplomb with which she delivered her gems. They thought her aim was to ridicule the whole educational process, and they applauded her courage.

Her reputation passed beyond the classroom walls. During recess, everyone in the school came to ask her classmates about "Plectrude's latest." Her heroic replies were like parts of an epic tale.

The conclusion was always the same:

"She's pushing it!"

"YOU'RE PUSHING IT, aren't you?" her father said angrily when he saw her report.

"I don't want to go to school anymore, papa. It's not for me."

"It can't go on like this!"

"I want to be a ballet dancer."

Her words didn't fall on deaf ears.

"She's right!" said Clémence.

"So you're defending her as well?"

71

"Of course! Our Plectrude's a genius at dancing! At her age she's got to devote herself to it body and soul! Why should she go on wasting her time with past participles?"

That same day, Clémence phoned the famous ballet school of the *petits rats* at the Paris Opéra.

THE TEACHERS AT the girl's dancing school were enthusiastic.

"We were hoping you'd decide to do this! She's made for it!"

They wrote letters of recommendation for Plectrude, speaking of her as a future Pavlova.

She was summoned in by the Opéra to take an exam. Clémence shrieked when the letter arrived, even though it meant nothing at all.

On the appointed day, Plectrude and her mother headed for the Opéra. Clémence's heart was pounding even harder than her child's when they reached the *école des rats*, the famous school itself.

Two weeks later, Plectrude received a letter admitting her to the school. It was the most joyful day of her mother's life.

In September, she would start at the Opéra School, where she would be a boarder. A great future was opening up before her.

This was April. Denis insisted that she finish the school year. "That way you'll be able to say you stopped in the ninth grade."

The child thought that this was both mean and ridiculous. Nonetheless, out of affection for her father, she stuck with it and passed. Now she was in good graces with everyone.

The whole school knew where she was going, and was very proud. Even the teachers who had thought Plectrude a nightmare declared that they had always sensed her genius.

The students praised her daring, the dinner ladies lauded her lack of appetite, the phys ed teacher (she had been dreadful at physical education) spoke of her suppleness and the delicacy of her muscles, and to cap it all, those who had never stopped hating her right from kindergarten prided themselves on being her friends.

The only member of the class whom the girl would have liked to impress showed nothing but polite admiration. If she had known Mathieu Saladin better, she would have known why his face was so impassive.

In fact, what he was thinking was, *Shit. I thought I had another five years to achieve my goal. Now she's going to be a star and I'm never going to see her again. If she were even a friend, I'd have an excuse to meet up with her. But she and I have never really become friends, and I'm not going to be like one of those jerks who pretend they adore a girl because they know what it will get them.*

On the last day of school, Mathieu Saladin bade Plectrude a cold farewell.

He's glad I'm leaving. She sighed. *I'm never going to see him again. Maybe I won't think about him so much.*

THAT SUMMER, THEY didn't go away on vacation. The *école des rats* was expensive. The phone never stopped ringing: a neighbor, an uncle, a friend, a colleague, wanted to come over and gaze upon this prodigy.

"And she's beautiful, too!" they exclaimed when they saw her.

Plectrude couldn't wait to go to boarding school so that she could get away from all this attention.

To escape the boredom, she ruminated on her amorous woes. She climbed to the top of her favorite cherry tree and closed her eyes. She told herself stories. The cherry tree became Mathieu Saladin.

She became aware of how foolish this was. *It's so stupid to be twelve and a half, and for everyone to like you except Mathieu Saladin!*

At night in her bed, the stories became far more intense: she and Mathieu Saladin were trapped in a barrel that was going over Niagara Falls. The barrel smashed open on some rocks, and she took turns pretending it was herself or Mathieu who had to be saved.

There was something to be said for both versions. She loved the thought of him diving to look for her at the bottom of the swirling water, wrapping her in his arms to bring her back to life, and then, on the shore, giving her mouth-to-mouth resuscitation. When he was the one who went over injured, she pulled him from the water, licking the blood from his wounds, rejoicing over the new scars that were going to make him even more handsome.

She felt shivers of desire.

SHE HAD WAITED for the new school year as though for liberation. It turned out to be incarceration.

She knew that the ballet school was run with an iron hand. But what she discovered there went far beyond what she had imagined.

Plectrude had always been the thinnest girl in every group. At the *école des rats* she was one of the "normal" ones. The "thin" ones would have been called skeletal anywhere else. Anyone who would have been considered to have commonplace proportions in the outside world was mocked as a fat cow within these walls.

On the first day, a kind of thin, old sausage-maker

examined the pupils as though they were cuts of meat. She separated them into three categories.

"Thin ones, you're fine. Stay like that. Normal ones, okay, but I've got my eye on you. Fat cows, either you lose weight or you go: there's no room for sows here."

These words were greeted with mirth by the thin ones. They looked like laughing corpses. *They're monstrous,* thought Plectrude.

One "fat cow," a pretty girl with a perfectly normal figure, burst into tears. The old woman came and yelled at her.

"There's no point sobbing in here. If you want to go on stuffing your fat face while hiding in your mother's skirts, no one's stopping you."

Then the young pieces of meat were weighed and measured. Plectrude, who was going to be thirteen in a month, was five feet two and weighed eighty-eight pounds, which wasn't much, especially since it was all muscle. Nonetheless, she was informed that her weight was a "maximum that should not be exceeded."

That first day at the *école des rats* persuaded all the girls that they had been brutally evicted from childhood. The previous day, their bodies had still been much-loved plants, watered and cherished. Growth was a marvelous natural phenomenon; their families were gardens where the soil was rich, and where life was gradual and nourishing. Suddenly they were uprooted from the moist earth, and replanted in a desiccated world, where the merciless eye of a hothouse plant expert decreed that a particular stem would have to be lengthened, a particular root would have to be lopped, and that this would happen whether they wanted it to or not.

Here, there was no tenderness in the eyes of the adults, just a scalpel to slice away the last flesh of childhood. The girls had traveled through time and space: in only a few seconds they had passed from the beginning of the second millennium in France to ancient China.

IT WOULD BE AN understatement to say that the school was ruled with an iron fist. Lessons began early in the morning and ended late at night, with barely noticeable interruptions for a meal unworthy of the name, and for short periods of study during which the girls savored the relaxation of their bodies so deeply that they forgot the intellectual effort involved.

Under this regimen, all the girls grew thin, including the ones already too thin. The latter, far from worrying about it, rejoiced. You could never be too skeletal.

But weight was not their chief concern. Their bodies were so exhausted by the endless hours of exercise that their sole obsession was to sit down. The moments when you didn't use your muscles seemed like miracles.

Plectrude waited to go to bed from the moment she got up. The moment she consigned her aching carcass to bed for the night was voluptuous. This was the only relaxation that the girls had. Meals brought anguish. The teachers had so demonized food that however mediocre it might have been, it appeared highly tempting. The girls were disgusted by the desire food aroused in them. A single mouthful was a mouthful too many.

Plectrude soon started wondering about things. She had come here to become a dancer, not to believe there was no higher ideal than sleep. She worked on her dancing from morning till evening, without a sense that dancing was what she was doing. She was like a writer forced to not write, but instead to study grammar incessantly. Of course, grammar is essential, but only if writing is the end in view: deprived of its purpose, grammar is but a sterile code. Plectrude had never felt less like a dancer than she had since coming to the *école des rats*. In the ballet classes that she had attended in previous years, there had been room for little choreographies. Here *all* they did was exercises. The barre started looking like the bars of a jail.

Her perplexity seemed to be shared by many of the

others. None of them spoke of it, yet they could all feel discouragement spreading among them.

Some girls left, and the school's staff seemed to have been hoping that they would. These defections led to others. This spontaneous shedding of surplus weight delighted the teachers. For poor Plectrude, each departure was like a death.

Inevitably, she was herself tempted to leave. What stopped her was her feeling that her mother would be angry with her, and that any reasons she gave would not be good enough.

It was clear that the staff was waiting for a predetermined list of people to leave, for their approach changed suddenly. The girls were called into a room larger than usual, and given a new speech.

"You may have noticed that many students have left the school over the last few weeks. We would not go as far as to say that we deliberately provoked them to go, but we will not be so hypocritical as to regret that they did."

There followed a silence, the sole purpose of which was to make the children uneasy.

"By leaving, those girls proved that they did not really want to dance. More precisely, they have shown that they lacked the patience a true dancer needs to have. Do you know what some of these silly geese said when they told us they were going? That they had come to dance, and that we did no dancing here. What on earth did they think? That they would be performing *Swan Lake* for us the day after tomorrow?"

Plectrude remembered an expression of her mother's: "retaliate first." The *école*'s teachers were busy retaliating first.

"Dancing is something you must earn. Dancing—dancing on a stage in front of an audience—is the greatest joy in the world. Even without the audience, even without the stage, dancing is absolute bliss. This is justification for the cruelest sacrifices. The education that we give you here shows dance for what it is: not the means, but the end. It would be immoral to allow pupils to dance when they hadn't earned the right. Eight hours a day at the barre and a famine diet will seem harsh only to those without sufficient desire to dance. Anyone who still wishes to leave, should go!"

NO ONE ELSE LEFT. The message had been loud and clear. You can accept the severest forms of discipline so long as they've been explained to you properly.

The reward came: they danced. To be sure, it wasn't much. But for the girls the mere fact of leaving the barre to launch themselves into the center of the room with everyone watching, to twirl around for a few moments and feel the extent to which their bodies had mastered their steps, was utterly intoxicating. If ten seconds could give so much pleasure, imagine what they would feel when they danced for two hours.

Plectrude felt sorry for Roselyne, who hadn't been accepted at the *école des rats*. She would only ever be an ordinary young girl for whom dancing would be a hobby. Plectrude blessed her teachers' harshness, for it had taught her that art was a religion.

What had shocked her before, seemed normal now. It seemed normal that they should be starved, that they should exhaust themselves at the barre, going over their technical exercises for hours at a stretch, that they should be insulted, that children without a hint of plumpness should be mocked as fat cows. It all seemed quite acceptable.

There were even worse things that initially had made Plectrude feel as though she was witnessing crimes against humanity, but now no longer revolted her. Those girls who displayed signs of puberty earlier than the others were forced to swallow pills that delayed certain changes. No one had periods at the *école,* not even in the upper classes.

She had had a secret talk about it with an older girl, who had told her, "For most students those pills aren't even necessary. Undernourishment is enough to obstruct the menstrual cycle and the physical changes that come with your first period. But some still manage to enter puberty in spite of this. They have to take the famous pill. You won't find a tampon in the whole school."

"Does anyone have their period in secret?"

"No way! They're the ones who ask for the pill."

At the time, Plectrude had been shocked by that conversation. Now she found the school's Spartan laws quite magnificent.

Her spirit had been subjugated, she was now beneath the teachers' yoke, she agreed with them on everything.

Fortunately, the voice of her childhood, still active and more knowledgeably rebellious than that of her adolescence, saved her by whispering healthily outrageous remarks. "Do you know why this place is called the *école des rats*? They say it's for the pupils, but it's really for the teachers. *They're* the rats—nasty rats with big teeth to gnaw the flesh from the bodies of the ballerinas. We, at least, deserve some credit for being passionate about dance. The only thing they're passionate about is ratting us out. They want to eat us up with sugar on top. Rats are misers, miserly about beauty, pleasure, life, and even dance! You think they love dance? They're its worst enemies! They're chosen for their hatred of dance, deliberately, because if they loved it, that would make life too much fun. Loving what your teacher loves would be too easy. They're asking something superhuman of us here: that we sacrifice ourselves to an art that our teachers hate, an art they betray a hundred times a day with their pettiness. Dance is all about spirit, grace, generosity, talent—the very opposite of the rat mentality."

The dictionary supplied her with nourishment. Plectrude read the "rat" entry with gusto: "gutter rat, dirty rat, rat-faced, rat fink." The school deserved its name.

There was careful deliberation involved in choosing the école's wretched teachers. The school believed, not without reason, that it would have been immoral to encourage the ballerinas. If it was to be total art, dance required the investment of the whole being. So the girls' motivation had to be tested by undermining their dreams down to their foundations. Those who gave in would never have the mentality of a star. Such methods, monstrous though they were, were based on sound principles.

But the teachers didn't know this. They were not aware of the supreme mission behind their sadism, and exercised it simply for its own sake.

And thus it was that, in secret, Plectrude also learned to dance against them.

WITHIN THREE MONTHS she lost eleven pounds. She was delighted. She also noted an extraordinary phenomenon: by passing below the symbolic bar of eighty-eight pounds, she hadn't merely lost weight, she had also lost her feelings.

Mathieu Saladin: the name that had once sent her into a trance now left her utterly indifferent. She hadn't seen the boy again, or had any news from him, so he hadn't been able to disappoint her. Nor had she met any other boys.

It wasn't the passage of time that had made her so cold. Three months wasn't long. She had been studying herself too closely not to notice the connection between cause and effect: every pound she lost took a part of her love with it. She didn't regret this. To be able to regret it, she would have had to have some feelings left. She was glad to be rid of this double burden: eleven pounds and a burning passion.

Plectrude vowed she would remember this great law: love, regret, desire, and infatuation were illnesses produced by bodies that weighed more than eighty-eight pounds.

If by some mischance she reached such obesity again

and feelings started tormenting her heart once more, she would know the remedy: stop eating.

Life was different when you weighed seventy-seven pounds. You focused all your time on mastering the physical ordeals of the day, distributing your energy in such a way as to have enough for eight hours of exercise, for confronting the temptations of mealtimes, and for proudly concealing your exhaustion—in other words, for dancing when you had earned the right.

Dancing was Plectrude's sole means of transcendence. It fully justified her arid existence. Putting your health at risk meant nothing at all so long as you could know the incredible sensation of taking flight.

THERE IS A WIDESPREAD misconception about classical dance. For many, it is merely a silly universe of tutus and pink slippers, *à pointe* mannerisms, and aerial soppiness. The worst thing is that it's true. Ballet *is* all those things.

But it isn't just those things. Strip ballet of its sentimental affectations, its tulle, its stuffiness, and its chignons, and you will discover that what remains is hugely important. The proof of this is that the best modern dancers come from the classical schools.

The Holy Grail of ballet is flight. No teacher would dream of putting it like that, for fear of sounding like a complete idiot. But anyone who has been taught the technique of the *sissone,* the *entrechat,* and the *grand jeté en avant,* knows beyond any doubt that what they are trying to teach is the art of flying.

The barre exercises are so tiresome because the barre is a perch. When you dream of taking off, when you can feel your limbs yearning to fly freely in the air, you are furious at being moored for hours on end to a piece of wood.

The barre corresponds to the training that fledglings receive in the nest: how to spread their wings before using them. For fledglings, a few hours is all it takes. But when a human being has the audacity to change species and learn to fly, she quite rightly needs to devote years of exhausting exercises to the effort.

She will be rewarded far beyond her expectations the moment she is allowed to leave the perch—the barre—and hurl herself into space. The spectator may not be able to see what happens in the body of the ballet dancer at that precise moment. What happens is the truest kind of madness. And the fact that this insanity adheres to a code does nothing to diminish the deranged aspect of the whole idea of classical ballet: that it is composed of a set of techniques designed to make human flight seem possible and reasonable. Consequently, why would anyone be surprised by the grotesquely gothic context in which this happens? Why should anyone expect that such a demented project be adopted by individuals of sound mind?

This lengthy digression is directed at those who would see ballet as nothing more than a source of entertainment. They are right to be amused. But let them also look beyond their amusement, for within classical dance lurks a fearsome ideal.

And the ravages that this ideal can wreak upon a young mind are like those of a hard drug.

AT CHRISTMAS, THEY went home for a short while.

No pupil at the *école des rats* looked forward to vacations with any great excitement. The whole prospect filled them all with apprehension. Holidays. What possible point could there be in those? They had been justifiable when life's purpose was pleasure, but that time—childhood—had come and gone. Now the sole meaning of their existence was dance. Family life, composed essentially of meals and flabbiness, was in direct contradiction to this.

Plectrude told herself that not looking forward to Christmas was another sign of leaving childhood. It was the first time that this had happened to her. She had been right about being afraid to turn thirteen. She had really changed.

Everyone noticed it. They were all struck by how thin she was. Only her mother was pleased. Denis, Nicole, Béatrice, and Roselyne, who had been invited over, all disapproved.

"You've got a face like a razor-blade."

"She's a dancer," protested Clémence. "You couldn't have expected her to come back to us with big round cheeks. You're very beautiful, my darling."

Apart from her thinness, a more profound change in Plectrude left them even more perplexed because they couldn't put a name to it. Perhaps it was so sinister that they simply didn't dare say what it was: Plectrude had lost her spirit. She had always been a laughing little girl, and now she seemed indifferent.

It must be the shock of coming home, Denis thought.

But the impression grew stronger with each passing day. Nothing she did could conceal her indifference.

Mealtimes seemed to be a torment for her. Her family was used to her eating very little; now she ate nothing at all, and the rest of the family felt tense.

Had they been able to see what was happening in Plectrude's head, they would have been even more worried than they were.

On the day of her arrival, they had all struck her as obese. Even Roselyne, a skinny adolescent, seemed enormous to her. She wondered how they could stand to have such huge bellies. She wondered how they could bear to lead such vain lives—great softness spreading everywhere, leading nowhere. She blessed her harsh existence and its privations. At least she was heading somewhere. It wasn't as if she was committed to the cult of suffering, but she did need meaning in her life. In that respect, Plectrude was already a teen-ager.

WHEN THEY WERE ALONE together, Roselyne, breath-less and excited, told her all about what had happened to her classmates. "And guess what? Well, Vanessa's go-ing out with Fred, yes, really, that senior!"

She was very quickly disappointed with her lack of success in getting any reaction.

"You were in their class for longer than I was—don't you care what's happening to them?"

"Don't take it the wrong way. If you knew how far all this is from me at the moment."

"Even Mathieu Saladin?" asked Roselyne.

"Of course," Plectrude said wearily.

"You didn't always feel like this."

"That's the truth."

"Are there any boys at your school?"

"No. They take their classes separately. We never see them."

"Just girls, then? What absolute hell!"

"We haven't got time to think about such things."

Plectrude didn't have the heart to tell her friend about the barrier separating those who weighed more than eighty-eight from those who weighed less, but she felt the truth of it now more than ever before. What did she care about those stupid high-school flirtations? She felt even sorrier for Roselyne now that her friend was wearing a bra.

"Do you want me to show you?"

"What?"

"My bra. You haven't stopped staring at it all the time I've been talking to you."

Roselyne lifted up her T-shirt. Plectrude shrieked with horror.

DEEP DOWN, THE GIRL who had learned to dance against her teachers also learned to live against her family. She said nothing, but she studied them critically. *They all slump! It's like they've been beaten down by the laws of gravity. Life has got to be better than that.*

She found that their lives, as opposed to her own, lacked poise, and she was ashamed on their behalf. Sometimes she wondered if she had been adopted.

. . .

"I TELL YOU IT WORRIES me. She's very thin," said Denis.

"So? She's a dancer," replied Clémence.

"Not all dancers are as thin as that."

"She's thirteen. It's normal at that age."

Reassured, Denis was able to get to sleep. The parental capacity for willful blindness is immense. By means of an observation—the frequent occurrence of thinness among adolescents—they manage to blot out individual circumstances. Their daughter may have been slender by nature, but this thinness wasn't natural.

The holidays came and went. Plectrude went back to school, to her very great relief.

"Sometimes I feel as though I've lost a child," said Denis.

"You're being selfish," protested Clémence. "She's happy."

She was wrong on both counts. First of all, the little girl was not happy. Secondly, her husband's selfishness was nothing compared to her own. She would so have liked to have been a ballerina, and Plectrude satisfied that ambition vicariously. So what if the health of her child needed to be sacrificed to that ideal. If anyone had said that to her, she would have opened her eyes wide and exclaimed, "All I want is for my daughter to be happy!"

Her reaction would have been an honest one. Parents don't know what remains concealed behind their own sincerity.

WHAT PLECTRUDE WAS experiencing at the *école des rats* was not the thing called happiness. Happiness requires a sense of security. The girl didn't sense the merest hint of that, and she was right not to: at this stage of her life, she was no longer playing with her health, she was gambling with it. She knew that.

What Plectrude was experiencing at the *école des rats* was called intoxication: ecstasy fed on a massive dose of obliviousness, obliviousness of privation, physical suffering, danger, and fear. Through such voluntary amnesia, she was able to throw herself into her dancing, and to know the mad illusion of it and the trance of flight.

She was becoming one of the school's best pupils. She was definitely not the thinnest of them, but she was without contest the most graceful. She possessed that marvelous ease of movement that is nature's most supreme injustice, for grace is given or withheld at birth, and no effort can compensate for its absence.

And then there was the fact that she was the prettiest of them all. Even at seventy-seven pounds, she didn't look like those corpses whose thinness the teachers praised. Her dancer's eyes lit up her face with their fantastic beauty. The teachers knew, without mentioning it to their pupils, that prettiness plays an enormously important part in the choosing of star dancers; in this respect, Plectrude was the most fortunate.

She was secretly worried about her health. She didn't talk to anyone about it, but at night her legs hurt so much that she had to stop herself from screaming. Although she knew nothing about medicine, she suspected the reason: she had cut all dairy products out of her diet. She actually noted that even a few spoonfuls of low-fat yogurt were enough to make her feel "bloated" (and what she meant by "bloated" may be hard for the rest of us to grasp).

Indeed, low-fat yogurt was the only form of lactose permitted in the school. Doing without it meant eliminating any intake of calcium, which cements adolescence. Sadistic as the adults at the school might have been, none of them recommended doing without yogurt, and even the most emaciated of them consumed it. Not Plectrude.

This deficiency very quickly led to atrocious pains

in her legs whenever she remained motionless for a few hours, as she did at night. To get rid of the pain she had to get up and move about. But the moment her legs started moving again came agonies worthy of a torture chamber. Plectrude had to bite on a rag to keep from crying out. Each time, she felt as though the bones in her calves and thighs were about to snap.

She realized that decalcification was the cause of her torment, but she couldn't bring herself to start eating that wretched yogurt again. Without knowing it, she was falling victim to the internal machinery of anorexia, which considers each fresh privation irreversible except at the cost of unendurable guilt.

She lost another four-and-a-half pounds, confirming her conviction that low-fat yogurt was "heavy." During the Easter vacation, her father told her she had turned into a skeleton. Her mother immediately went into raptures about her daughter's beauty. Clémence was the only member of the family Plectrude was still happy to see. *At least* she *understands me.* Her sisters, and even Roselyne, looked upon her as a stranger. They didn't feel anything in common with that assemblage of bones.

Since dropping below seventy-three pounds, the dancer had even fewer emotions than before. Their rejection of her caused her no pain.

. . .

PLECTRUDE ADMIRED HER LIFE. She felt as though she was alone in her battle against gravity. She waged war upon it armed with fasting and dance.

The Grail was flight and Plectrude was the most likely, of all her fellow knights, to attain it. What did pain matter in the face of the immensity of her quest?

The months and years passed. The dancer was integrated within her school like a Carmelite within her order. There would be no salvation outside its walls.

She was the rising star, discussed at the highest levels. She knew that.

At the age of fifteen, she still measured five foot two, which meant that she hadn't grown so much as an inch since entering the *école des rats*. Her weight: seventy pounds.

It sometimes seemed to her that she had had no life before this. She hoped that her existence would never change. Other people's admiration, whether real or imagined, was emotionally satisfying enough.

She knew too that her mother loved her to distraction. Although she didn't show it, awareness of that love served as her spinal column. One day, she mentioned the leg problem to Clémence. "How brave you are," was all her mother said.

Plectrude savored the compliment, although deep inside she had the sense that her mother should have said something very different. What, she didn't know.

THE INEVITABLE HAPPENED. One November morning, when Plectrude had just got out of bed, biting her rag so as not to howl with pain, she collapsed. She heard a cracking noise in her thigh.

She couldn't move. She called for help. She was sent to the hospital.

A doctor who hadn't seen her before studied her X rays.

"How old is this woman?"

"Fifteen."

"What? She's got the bones of a menopausal sixty-year-old!"

They asked her some questions. She told them straight out that she hadn't had any dairy products since she was thirteen—the age when the body craves them.

"Are you anorexic?"

"No, of course not!" she exclaimed with sincerity.

"Do you think weighing sixty-five pounds at your age is normal?"

"Seventy pounds!" she protested.

"What difference do you think that makes?"

She resorted to Clémence's arguments. "I'm a ballerina. It's better not to have curves."

"I didn't know they'd started recruiting dancers from the concentration camps."

"How dare you insult my school!"

"So what do you think about a place where a teenager is allowed to self-destruct? I'm going to call the police," said the doctor stoutly.

Plectrude instinctively leapt to the defense of her order.

"No! It's my fault! I stopped eating it in secret! No one knew."

"No one wanted to know. The result is that you've broken your tibia just by falling on the ground. If you were normal, a month in a cast would do it. In your condition, I don't know how many months you're going to have to keep it on. Not to mention the rehab you'll have to go through afterwards."

"Does that mean I'm not going to be able to dance for a long time?"

"My dear girl, you'll never be able to dance again."

Plectrude's heart stopped. She sank into a kind of coma.

SHE EMERGED FROM IT a few days later. She passed through that exquisite moment when you recall nothing, then she remembered the sentence passed on her. A nurse with a pleasant manner confirmed it.

"Your bones are seriously weakened, especially in your legs. Even when your tibia is mended, you won't be able to start dancing again. The slightest jump, the slightest impact could bruise you. It will take years to bring your calcium levels back up to normal."

Telling Plectrude that she wouldn't dance again was like telling Napoleon he wouldn't have an army again. She was being deprived not of her vocation, but of her destiny.

She couldn't believe it. She interrogated every doctor she could. Not one gave her the faintest glimmer of hope. They should be credited for that. If even one of them had given her a hundredth of a chance of recovery, she would have clung to it, fatally.

Plectrude was surprised that Clémence hadn't come to her bedside. She asked to make a phone call. Her father told her that when the terrible news had come, her mother had fallen seriously ill.

"She's running a fever, she's delirious. She thinks she's you. She keeps saying, 'I'm only fifteen, my dream can't be over yet, I'm going to be a dancer, I can't be anything but a dancer!' "

The idea of Clémence being in pain was the final straw for Plectrude. From her bed, she studied the intravenous drip that was feeding her. She became convinced that it was injecting her with unhappiness in the guise of food.

WHILE SHE WAS forbidden to make the slightest movement, Plectrude remained in the hospital. Her father sometimes came to visit her. She asked him why her mother didn't come with him.

"She's still too ill," he replied.

This went on for several months. Aside from her father, no one came to see her, no one from the *école des rats,* or from her family, or from her former school. It was as though Plectrude no longer belonged to any world.

She spent her days doing absolutely nothing. She didn't want to read anything. She refused to watch television. She was diagnosed as suffering from deep depression.

She couldn't swallow anything. A good thing she had her IV. But it disgusted her: it was what connected her with life, in spite of herself.

WHEN SPRING CAME, she was taken to see her parents. Her heart pounded at the idea of seeing her mother again, but her wish was refused. "But why not? Is she dead?"

"No, she's alive, but she doesn't want you to see her in this state."

It was more than Plectrude could bear. She waited until her sisters were at school and her father had gone out, then she got out of her bed. She was able to move around on crutches.

She reached her parents' bedroom, where Clémence was sleeping. When she saw her mother, the girl thought she was dead. Her complexion was ashen, and she seemed even thinner than her daughter. Plectrude collapsed at her side, weeping, "Mama! Mama!"

The sleeping woman woke up and said, "You're not allowed in here."

"But I had to see you. And anyway I've done it now, and it's better that way. I'd rather know how you are. As long as you're alive, nothing else matters. You're going to start eating. You'll get better. We're both going to get better, Mama."

She noticed that her mother was still cold, and that she wasn't reaching out to hold her.

"Hold me! I so need you!"

Clémence remained inert.

"Poor Mama, you're too weak even for that."

She stood up and looked at her mother. How she had changed! There was no longer any warmth in her eyes. Something within her had died. Plectrude didn't want to understand it.

Mama thinks she's me. She's stopped eating because I stopped eating. If I eat, she will eat. If I get better, she'll get better.

The girl dragged herself to the kitchen and found a bar of chocolate. Then she went back to Clémence's bedroom and sat on the bed.

"Look, Mama. I'm eating."

The chocolate was a shock to her mouth, which was no longer used to food, let alone such a rich confection. Plectrude forced herself not to reveal her nausea.

"It's milk chocolate, Mama. It's full of calcium. It's good for me."

So this was what eating was? Her organs shuddered, her stomach revolted. She fell to her knees and vomited.

Humiliated, disconsolate, Plectrude remained motionless, contemplating her work.

It was then that her mother said, dryly, "You disgust me."

The girl looked at the glacial eye of the woman who said this. She didn't want to believe what she had heard and seen. She fled as quickly as her crutches allowed.

. . .

PLECTRUDE FELL ON HER BED and sobbed her heart out. Eventually she fell asleep.

When she woke up, she felt a strange sensation: hunger.

She asked Béatrice, who had come back in the meantime, to bring her a tray.

"Victory!" applauded her sister, who brought her some bread, cheese, jam, ham, and chocolate.

The girl refused the chocolate, but she devoured the rest.

Béatrice exulted.

Plectrude's appetite had returned. This was not bulimia, but healthy, ravenous hunger. She ate three hearty meals a day, feeling particularly attracted to cheese, as though her body were communicating its most urgent needs. Her father and her sisters were delighted.

She quickly put on weight. She regained her eighty-eight pounds and her beautiful face. Everything was for the best. She even managed not to feel guilty, which, for a former anorexic, is really quite extraordinary.

As she had predicted, her recovery meant her mother's recovery as well. Clémence finally left her room and saw her daughter again, not having so much as glimpsed her since the day she had vomited. She looked at Plectrude in consternation. "You've gotten fatter!"

"Yes, Mama," stammered the girl.

"You were so pretty before!"

"Don't you think I'm pretty like this?"

"No, you're fat."

"But Mama! I weigh eighty-eight pounds!"

"Exactly: you've put on eighteen pounds."

"I had to!"

"That's what you say to ease your conscience. It was calcium you needed, not weight. You don't look like a dancer now!"

"But Mama, I can't dance anymore. I'm not a dancer anymore. Do you know how much pain I'm in?"

"If you were in pain, you wouldn't be so hungry."

The worst was the hard voice with which the woman delivered her verdict.

"Why do you talk like that? I'm your daughter!"

"You've never been my daughter."

CLÉMENCE TOLD HER everything: Lucette, Fabien, Fabien's murder by Lucette, her birth in prison, Lucette's suicide.

"What are you saying?" moaned Plectrude.

"Ask your father—or rather, your uncle—if you don't believe me."

Once over her initial shock, the girl managed to ask, "Why are you telling me this today?"

"I was going to have to tell you some day, wasn't I?"

"Why in such a cruel way? You've always been a wonderful mother. Now you're talking to me as though I had never been your daughter."

"Because you've betrayed me. You know how much I dreamt of you being a dancer."

"I had an accident! It wasn't my fault."

"Yes, it was your fault! If you hadn't stupidly decalcified yourself!"

"I told you about the pains in my legs!"

"That's not true!"

"Yes it is, I talked to you about it! You even congratulated me on my courage."

"You're lying!"

"I don't lie! Do you think it's normal for a mother to congratulate her daughter on having pains in her legs? It was a cry for help, and you didn't hear it."

"That's right, say it's all my fault."

Plectrude was speechless.

HER WORLD COLLAPSED. She had no future, no family, nothing.

Denis was kind, but weak. Clémence told him to

stop praising Plectrude for regaining her appetite. "Don't encourage her to get fat, for heaven's sake!"

"She's not fat," he bleated. "A little plump, maybe."

That phrase, "a little plump," told the girl that she had lost an ally.

Telling a fifteen-year-old girl that she's fat, or even "a little plump," when she weighs eighty-eight pounds, is the same as telling her not to grow up.

Faced with a disaster of this scale, a girl has only two choices: fall back into anorexia, or bulimia. Miraculously, Plectrude didn't succumb to either. Her appetite, which any doctor would have considered healthy, and which Clémence declared to be "monstrous," continued to grow.

In fact, Plectrude's body was telling her to be hungry: she had years to catch up on. Thanks to her frenetic consumption of cheese she grew an inch and a half. Nonetheless, for an adult, five foot three and a half was better than five foot two.

WHEN SHE WAS SIXTEEN she had her first period. She told Clémence as though it were a marvelous piece of news. Clémence shrugged her shoulders contemptuously.

"Aren't you happy that I'm finally normal?"

"How much do you weigh?"

"A hundred pounds."

"That's what I thought. You're obese."

"A hundred pounds, five foot three and a half. That's obese?"

"Face the facts. You're enormous."

Plectrude, who had regained the full use of her legs, went and threw herself on her bed. She didn't cry, she felt a pang of hatred that lasted for hours. She struck her pillow with her fist. An inner voice howled, "She wants to kill me! My mother wants me dead!"

She had never stopped thinking of Clémence as her mother. She was her mother because she was the one who had really given her life—and now she wanted to take it away.

In her place, many teenagers would have committed suicide, but the survival instinct was deeply rooted in Plectrude. She got up, saying in a loud, calm voice, "I won't let myself be killed, Mama."

SHE TOOK HER OWN life in hand, insofar as that is possible for a sixteen-year-old girl who has lost everything. Since her mother had gone mad, she would be an adult in her place.

She signed up for drama classes. She made a great

impression. Her first name helped. Being called "Plec-trude" was a double-edged blade: either you were ugly and the name emphasized your ugliness, or you were beautiful and it increased your beauty a hundredfold.

The latter was true in her case. People were already struck when they saw that girl with the wonderful eyes and the dancer's grace entering a room. When they learned her first name, they looked at her even more closely, and admired her sublime hair, her tragic expression, her perfect mouth, her ideal complexion.

Her drama teacher told her she had a "physique" (She thought it was a strange expression. Didn't everyone have a "physique"?) and advised her to start going to casting calls.

That was how she came to be selected to play the part of the teenage Geraldine Chaplin in a television film. When Chaplin saw her, the actress exclaimed, "I wasn't as beautiful as that at her age!", but there was an undeniable similarity between their thin faces.

That kind of role brought Plectrude some income but, unfortunately, not enough of one to help her get away from her mother, which was her intention. In the evening she went home as late as possible, so as not to bump into Clémence. But she wasn't always able to avoid her, and was always greeted with something like "Hey! Here comes the fat girl!"

That was if she was lucky. The worst was, "Evening, Blubber!"

It would be hard to express how hurtful such comments were, or the air of disgust with which they were delivered.

One day, Plectrude dared to reply that Béatrice, who weighed sixteen pounds more than she did, never got such insults. To which her mother replied, "That's irrelevant, as you know very well."

She wasn't bold enough to say, no, she didn't know very well. All she knew was that her sister was allowed to be normal, and she wasn't.

ONE EVENING, WHEN PLECTRUDE had been unable to find an excuse not to have dinner with her family, and when Clémence gave a scornful expression every time her daughter swallowed a mouthful of food, she finally protested, "Mama, stop looking at me like that! Haven't you ever seen anyone eating before?"

"It's for your own good, my darling. I'm worried about your bulimia."

"Bulimia!"

Plectrude stared at her father, then at her sisters. "You're all too cowardly to defend me!"

Her father stammered, "No, I . . . It doesn't bother me if you've got a good appetite."

"You're such a coward!" cried the girl. "I eat less than you do."

Nicole shrugged her shoulders.

"I couldn't care less."

"Oh, you're such a caring sister!" screeched Plectrude.

Béatrice took a deep breath. "Okay, Mama. Maybe you can leave my sister in peace, all right?"

"Thank you," said Plectrude.

Clémence smiled. "She's not your sister, Béatrice."

"What are you talking about?"

"Do you think this is the right moment?" murmured Denis.

Clémence got up and went to get a photograph, which she threw on the table.

"This is Lucette, my sister, Plectrude's real mother."

As she told Nicole and Béatrice the story, Plectrude grabbed the photograph and stared at the dead woman's pretty face.

The sisters were flabbergasted.

"I look like her," said Plectrude.

She remembered that Lucette had committed suicide at the age of nineteen, and realized that that would be her fate, too. *I'm sixteen. Another three years to live, and a child to bring into the world.*

• • •

FROM THAT MOMENT ONWARD Plectrude looked at all the many boys who buzzed around her with different eyes. She couldn't stare at one without thinking, *Would I like to have his baby?*

More often than not, the answer was no. The idea of having a child with one of these preening young men seemed unthinkable to her.

In her drama classes, the teacher decided that Plectrude and one of her fellow students would perform a scene from Eugène Ionesco's *The Bald Soprano*. The girl was so taken by the play that she got hold of Ionesco's complete works. She suddenly discovered that rage to read that keeps you up for whole nights at a time.

She had tried to read before, but the books always fell from her hands. It may be that within the universe of the written word is a work that will turn each person into a reader, should fate allow that to happen. What Plato says about the loving half—that other part of us floating around somewhere, and which must be found if we are not to remain incomplete until our dying day—is even more true where books are concerned.

Ionesco is my author, Plectrude thought. This gave her considerable happiness, the kind of intoxication that can only come from discovering a book that you love.

For some people, that first literary passion leads to a love of reading. This was not the case with our heroine, who only looked at other books to confirm how boring they were. She decided she wouldn't read anyone else's words, and prided herself on her loyalty.

One evening, when she was watching television, Plectrude saw some footage of the French chanteuse Catherine Ringer. Listening to her sing, Plectrude felt a mixture of infatuation and bitterness: infatuation because she thought Ringer's voice was amazing; bitterness because she would have liked to sing like that herself, but she had no way of learning how.

Had she been the kind of girl who had a different dream every week, it wouldn't have mattered so much. But this was not the case. Plectrude didn't go through crazes. Her drama classes didn't thrill her. She would have sold her soul to dance again, but the doctors, though observing a definite progress in her recalcification, were unanimous in forbidding her to return to her old vocation.

The discovery of Catherine Ringer was a shock because for the first time Plectrude had a dream that had nothing at all to do with ballet.

She consoled herself with the thought that she was going to die in two years anyway, and that before then she had to bring a child into the world. *I don't have time to be a singer.*

ONE OF HER ASSIGNMENTS in her drama classes was to act out a passage from Ionesco's *The Lesson.* For an actor, getting one of the main roles in a play by your favorite author is like Byzantium and Cythera, Rome and the Vatican: having your cake and eating it, too.

It wouldn't be accurate to say that she *became* the young pupil in the play, for she had always been that girl—so passionate about what she apprenticed herself to that she destroyed whatever it was—aided and abetted by a teacher who chews up knowledge and students.

She endowed her role with such a sense of the sacred that it infected the other role. It was left up to her as to who would play the part of the teacher.

During a rehearsal, in response to a line miraculous in its truthfulness ("Philology leads to crime"), she told him that she wanted him to be the father of her child. He thought this was perfectly in keeping with the spirit of Ionesco and agreed. That night, she took him at his word.

A month later, Plectrude knew that she was pregnant: a warning to anyone who still sees Ionesco only as a comic writer.

. . .

PLECTRUDE WAS THE SAME age as her mother had
been when she gave birth. The baby was called Simon.
He was beautiful and healthy.

She felt a fabulous surge of love when she saw him.
She hadn't expected that she would have such a strong
maternal instinct, and she was sorry about it. "Suicide's
not going to be easy."

She was nonetheless determined to take things to
their conclusion. *I've already made concessions to fate by
deciding not to kill Simon's father. But I'm not going to get
myself out of it.*

She rocked the child, murmuring, "I love you, Simon, I love you. I'll die because I must. If I could
choose, I would stay near you. But I must die. It's an
order, I can feel it."

A week later, she said to herself, *It's now or never. If I
go on living, I'm going to get too attached to Simon. The
longer I wait, the harder it's going to be.*

She didn't write a letter, for the simple reason that
she didn't like writing. What she was about to do
didn't require further explanation.

Feeling her resolve weaken, she decided to put on
her finest clothes. She had noted that elegance tended

to inspire. Two years previously, at a flea market, she had found a dress that looked as if it had once belonged to some grand duchess. It was midnight blue with old lace, so sumptuous that it was almost unwearable.

If I don't wear it today, I'll never wear it, she reflected, before bursting out laughing as she realized how profoundly true that was.

Pregnancy had left her a little thinner, and she floated in her dress, but she made the best of it. She let down her magnificent hair, which fell to the small of her back. She made herself up to look like a tragic fairy. She was pleased, telling herself that now she could kill herself without shame.

PLECTRUDE KISSED SIMON. The moment she left her apartment she wondered how she was going to do it. Throw herself under a train, in front of a car, or into the Seine? *I'll just see,* she concluded. *If you worried about that sort of detail you'd never do anything.*

She walked to the nearest station, but didn't have the courage to throw herself under the wheels of the suburban line. *Where dying's concerned, it would be best to do it in the middle of the city, and in the least awful way,* she said to herself, with a certain sense of propriety. So she got on the train. No one could ever remember having seen a passenger like Plectrude, who was smiling beatifically. The prospect of suicide put her in an excellent mood.

She went into the center of the city and walked along the Seine, in search of the bridge best suited to her undertaking. She couldn't make her mind up between the Pont Alexandre III, the Pont des Arts, and the Pont-Neuf, so she walked around for a long time, going over their respective merits in her mind.

In the end she decided the Pont Alexandre III was too magnificent, and the Pont des Arts too intimate. The Pont-Neuf seduced her because it was both old and had semicircular platforms, ideally suited for last-minute changes of mind.

People turned their heads at the sight of this beautiful woman. She was too absorbed in her project to notice. Never since childhood had Plectrude felt so euphoric.

She sat down on the edge of the bridge, her feet dangling over the void. Many people sat like this, and it didn't attract attention. She looked around her. A gray sky hung over Notre Dame, the surface of the Seine rippled in the wind. Suddenly Plectrude was struck by the great age of the world. How quickly her nineteen years would be swallowed up in the centuries of Paris!

She felt dizzy, and her exaltation subsided. The grandeur of durable things, the eternity that she wouldn't be a part of! She had brought a child into the world who wouldn't remember her. Apart from that, nothing. The only person she had loved was her mother and by killing herself, she would be obeying the mother she no longer loved. *That's not true. There's Simon as well. I love him. But given how destructive a mother's love is, it would be better if I spared him that.*

Below her legs, the river beckoned.

Why have I waited for this moment to feel what it is that I lack? My life has been racked with hunger and thirst. Nothing's ever nourished me—my heart has dried up, my mind is starving, and I've got a gaping hole where my soul should be. Is this how I'll die?

The void roared around her. The question crushed her. She was tempted to escape it by letting her feet become heavier than her brain.

At that very moment came a voice, a distant yell. "Plectrude!"

Is that a voice from among the living or the dead? she wondered.

She leaned toward the water, as though she would see someone in it.

The shout doubled in intensity. "Plectrude!"

A man's voice.

She turned toward where it was coming from.

THAT DAY, MATHIEU SALADIN had felt an inexplicable need to walk along the Seine.

He was making the best of the mild, gray day, when he saw an apparition approaching him: a girl of dazzling beauty dressed for a ball.

He stopped to watch her pass. She didn't see him. She didn't see anyone, with her big, astounding eyes. Then he recognized her. He smiled with joy: *I've found her! This time I'm not going to let her go.*

He followed her and felt that pleasure that comes from secretly following someone you know, observing their behavior, interpreting their actions.

She turned onto the Pont-Neuf. He knew its reputation as a bridge for suicides, but he wasn't worried. She didn't look desperate. He rested his elbows on the railing along the Seine and leaned forward to watch his former classmate.

Gradually it occurred to him that Plectrude was behaving very oddly. Her joyful look struck him as suspicious. He knew suddenly that she was going to throw herself in the river. He yelled her name and ran toward her.

• • •

SHE RECOGNIZED HIM immediately.

"Are you with anybody?" asked Mathieu, not wasting a second.

"Single, with a baby," she replied, just as crisply.

"Perfect. Want me?"

"Yes."

He gripped Plectrude's hips and swung them around one hundred and eighty degrees so that her feet weren't dangling over the void. They tongue-wrestled for a moment to seal what had been said.

"You weren't going to kill yourself, by any chance?"

"No," she replied, out of modesty.

He locked lips with her again. She thought, *A minute ago I was about to throw myself into the void, and now I'm in the arms of the man of my life, a man I haven't seen for seven years, whom I thought I'd never see again. I'll put off my death until later.*

PLECTRUDE DISCOVERED A SURPRISING thing: you could be happy once you'd reached adulthood.

"I'm going to show you where I live," Mathieu Saladin said.

"You don't waste any time!"

"I've wasted seven years. That's enough."

If Mathieu Saladin had had any idea what this admission would unleash upon him, he'd have kept his trap shut. Over and over, Plectrude shouted at him, "*You* made *me* wait seven years! *You* made *me* suffer!"

To which Mathieu protested, "You left me, too, you know! Why didn't you tell me you loved me when we were twelve?"

"The boy's supposed to do that," Plectrude said bossily.

One day, when Plectrude was launching off on the familiar refrain, "*You* made *me* wait seven years!" Mathieu told her something new.

"You're not the only one who's been in a hospital. Between the age of twelve and eighteen I was hospitalized six times."

"What? Is this some new excuse? And for what trivial ailment, pray, were you being treated?"

"To be more precise, between the age of one and eighteen I was hospitalized eighteen times."

She frowned.

"It's a long story," he began.

AT THE AGE OF one, Mathieu Saladin had died.

Baby Mathieu Saladin was crawling around his parents' living room, exploring the exciting universe of the feet of armchairs and the undersides of tables. An extension cord plugged into an electrical socket caught his attention. The baby followed the cord to its end—a captivating plastic bulb. He put it in his mouth and salivated. He received a shock that killed him.

Mathieu's father immediately drove the baby to the hospital, where the best doctor in the world brought the little body back to life.

But he still had to be given a mouth. Mathieu Saladin no longer had anything that might have merited the name: no lips, no palate. The doctor sent him to the best surgeon in the universe, who took a little bit of cartilage here, a bit of skin there, and, at the end of his painstaking patchwork, reconstructed, if not a mouth, at least the resemblance of one.

"That's all I can do for now," he concluded. "Come back in a year."

Every year he performed a new operation on Mathieu Saladin. And every year he said goodbye with the same two sentences. This ritual became a family joke.

Plectrude listened to him with rapt attention.

"That's why you've got that sublime scar on your moustache?"

"Sublime?"

"There's nothing more beautiful!"

These two creatures were destined for each other.

During their first year of life, each had come far too close to death.

A FEW YEARS PASSED. Experiencing perfect love with Mathieu Saladin, a musician, had given Plectrude the courage to become a singer, under the pseudonym "Robert." The name of a popular French dictionary, it was ideally suited to the encyclopedic dimensions of her suffering.

In most cases the greatest misfortunes assume the face of friendship: Plectrude met Amélie Nothomb and saw in her the friend, the sister that she so needed.

Plectrude told her about her life. Amélie listened with alarm to this tragic tale. She asked Plectrude if so many attempts to murder her hadn't given her the desire to kill.

"Your father was murdered by your mother when she was eight months pregnant with you. We're sure that you were awake, because you had the hiccups. So you're a witness!"

"But I didn't see anything!"

"You must have been aware of something. You're a very special kind of witness: a witness *in utero*. They say that babies in their mothers' bellies hear music and know when their parents are making love. Your

121

mother emptied a gun into your father: you must have felt it, one way or another."

"Where are we going with this, exactly?"

"You're saturated with that murder. Let's not even talk about the metaphorical attempted murders of you, and those you've committed against yourself. How could you not have become a murderess?"

Plectrude, who would never have thought of that, could think of nothing else afterwards. She satisfied her murderous impulse upon the very person who had suggested it. She took a rifle and fired it at Amélie's temple.

"It's the only way I could get her to shut up," she told her husband curtly.

Plectrude and Mathieu looked at the corpse with tears in the corners of their eyes. From that point on their life became an Ionesco play: *Amélie or How to Get Rid of It.*

Murder and sex are often followed by the same question: what should we do with the body?

Plectrude and Mathieu still haven't decided.